UNWANTED:

ABANDONED BUT NEVER BROKEN

BY

SARAH MITCHELL

v25-0328

Acknowledgements

I want to thank a few people for helping me on this journey. My family Ian, Jacob, Abigail and Mackenzie: I could not have completed this project without your help and encouragement. Thank you!!! You are the four people I want most to be proud of me.

Holly, Terry, Donnette and Fred: Your unconditional love has changed my life. Thank you!

To the grammar Goddesses, Elayne Masters, Melissa Aird and Susan Schader: Thank you for teaching me all about grammar and convincing me that I could do this.

My editor, Patricia Alexander: Thank you for being the last set of sharp eyes on this manuscript.

And Brian Schwartz: Thank you for helping me turn this manuscript into a book.

Chapter 1

"Do you understand that by signing this you are giving your daughter to the state of California?" I heard my caseworker, Darlene, say through the door. With my only belongings shoved into the grocery bag at my feet, I sat quietly outside her office.

"I never wanted her." There was no hesitation in my mother's voice.

We didn't look at each other when she walked past me. What was the point? I had spent 15 years being reminded that my blue eyes were nothing but a painful memory. A product of rape. Why would she want me? Why would anyone want me? As she reached the main door, I glanced up.

"Stacy. What are you going to do with my little sisters?"

She paused for a second—her long, mousy-brown hair still in motion—took a breath, and walked out of the building that I would now call home.

When a hand touched my shoulder, my whole body tensed.

"Follow me, Samantha," Darlene said softly.

I picked up my bag, slowly stood up, and followed her through a set of double doors, eying the tall, thin lady in her fancy grey pantsuit.

Bet she doesn't shop at Goodwill.

The doors swung shut and, with a loud click, locked behind me. It took me a minute to get used to the smell. It wasn't a bad smell, just like someone had recently cleaned the entire place with hand sanitizer.

We paused at the end of a door-lined hall that opened into a huge sitting room painted light blue. The carpet was clean, but worn areas created paths across the room. The opening song to *Gilligan's Island* was playing on a small TV in the far corner where some teens were hanging out. A few boys were shooting pool on a scruffy, old table in the middle of the room. All the doors around the room were closed except one at the opposite end of the TV area.

A couple of kids walked out holding juice cups, so I figured the kitchen must be back there. I wondered what was behind the other doors. Several girls were scattered around a cluster of light-blue couches that faced where my caseworker had left me standing. I could tell they were trying not to look my way, but they were losing the battle.

When I realized they were sizing me up, it hit me that my clothes were two sizes too big.

I will not cry. I will not let anyone see me break.

A short, round lady in purple scrubs came over and ordered me to follow her. A faint shuffling sound came from her thighs rubbing together as she walked. Her short, bobbed hair bounced with each step. All eyes were on me as I walked across the room to another hall. I felt someone next to me and jumped, snapping my head to the right. Darlene had joined us.

"What's with all the stinkin' blue?" I asked.

Darlene snickered. "Research shows that blue is calming. I realize this is all strange for you, Sam, but give it a chance. At least I know you'll be safe here."

When we walked through an open doorway, the nurse said, "This is your room. Empty your bag onto the bed on the right. I have to search your items."

I hesitated, wondering if I could make a break for it. Then, remembering the doors that locked behind me, I sighed inwardly and dumped out what my mother had allowed me to take. The nurse glanced over my one pair of jeans, two pairs of socks, two pair of underpants and two shirts.

Her expression softened. "Dear, I am Melanie." She sat on the bed and continued, "I need to check your person, too."

I took a step back, instantly feeling clammy.

Don't touch me.

Melanie looked at Darlene and then back at me. "Are you okay?"

I stiffened but nodded weakly and cringed as she ran her hands down me.

She lifted up my shirt and slid it back down without making eye contact. I pulled out my front pockets to show that they were empty, then took the photo of my two little sisters from my back pocket.

"This is all I have," I whispered, more for myself than for her. The warning glare in my eye made it clear I wasn't about to let her take it.

She handed me a rulebook, *New Life Treatment Center for Problem Adolescents* stamped on the cover in big, black letters. I took a deep breath and let it out slowly.

"You can put your items in there," Melanie stated, pointing towards a dresser. Then the two women were gone and I was alone.

I could tell by looking at the other bed that I had a roommate. It was unmade, with a teddy bear sitting on a pillow. Across from both beds was a dresser. Taped above my roommate's dresser were unframed photos of what looked like friends and ragged-edged pictures of the ocean torn from magazines. A few stacked paperbacks and a handmade necklace sat neatly on top.

I tossed my stuff in the top drawer of my dresser and put my photo back in my pocket. If I could find a way to make a run for it, the photo of my sisters was going with me.

The small bathroom was clearly for just the two of us. There was a sink with a mirror above it. No shower? I looked in the mirror, staring deep into the eyes of the person looking back. My long, brown, untamed hair framed my naturally pale skin.

Even though I knew the answer, I whispered to the girl in the mirror, "What is so horrible about you? What could be so horrible that the one person who is supposed to love you no matter what hates you?"

Most of the times my mother looked at me, she would grumble, "There are those eyes. You have *his* eyes," as if it was a curse. I tried not to think about the other things she told me, the details of the abortion she tried to give herself or the pain of carrying and then delivering something she feared.

A girl wearing a black T-shirt and torn jeans walked in through the open door. Her wild, curly red hair was down to the middle of her back. She looked me over and stepped to her side of the room. We stared in silence at each other for a minute.

"You the new girl?" Her eyes were sea-glass green.

I wanted to say "Duh!" but decided that wasn't polite. "Yeah. I'm Sam."

"Tara. Ain't so bad here. It's almost dinnertime, so you better get ready. They pass out meds before we eat."

"I don't take meds," I told her matter-of-factly.

She rolled her eyes and smiled. "Not yet. Want a tour?" she asked walking towards the door. I shrugged but followed.

"This is the girls' hall," she continued, her arms waving above her head as she walked. "The boys' rooms are in this area, then the sitting or meeting room and kitchen is at the end of the hall. Washer and dryer are in the sitting room. You must have a full load to wash though." She walked into the kitchen and sat down.

Well, guess the tour is over. Guess I'll go back to our room.

After dinner, we had free time. A nurse announced we had 15 minutes to get ready for bed. Everyone scattered, some went to the kitchen and grabbed a juice out of the fridge. Tara and I went straight to our room, brushed our teeth, then Tara put on PJ's and got into bed. A nurse came to the door, so I jumped under the covers.

"Tara and Sam, night, ladies!" she shut off our light and closed the door. The only light that filled our room now was coming in from the rectangle-shaped window in our door. Minutes later, that light dimmed.

It was dark in there and my stomach rumbled.

"Logan? Is there any water left?" I whispered.

"No. Nothing left," he whispered back.

"Do you think your dad will come back?" I barely asked. He didn't answer.

The footsteps were getting heavier...closer. Someone was in the house. We froze. The rattle of keys made us move to the back of the closet. Suddenly, light filled the space and someone grabbed my shoulder.

"Sam ... Sam ... Wake up!"

I abruptly flew up out of bed to get away from the hand shaking me. Tara stared at me before saying, "You were dreaming."

I nodded and watched her climb back in bed. I went into the bathroom and closed the door, careful not to look in the mirror as I cupped water in my hands and dunked my face in it.

Logan's dad never came back.

"Samantha, time to wake up." Melanie was leaning over me; the bright beam of her flashlight making me blink.

"Is it morning?" I groaned.

"Almost. Nurse Steven needs to draw blood, then you can go back to sleep," Melanie said quietly, clicking on the light above my bed.

My eyes shot open. "You're not stabbing me with a needle. No way!" Tara laughed and rolled over.

"Your doctor ordered blood work. We're here to collect it," Melanie repeated, sounding annoyed.

"What doctor? I don't have a doctor," I stated and demanded to talk to this "doctor" who wanted my blood.

"Dr. Sue won't be in till noon, and you can't eat until we have your blood drawn," Melanie snapped.

"I'm not hungry. I'll wait to see her."

Melanie pulled the cord on the light above me and left with a huff.

What were they thinking? Like I would just let them take my blood? I jumped out of bed and dug out the rulebook that I had tossed in my drawer. *Where does it say they can take my blood?*

Melanie made me stay in my room until everyone was at breakfast. "Follow me, Sam," she said crisply, opening my door, then turning to walk away. We reached the end of the girl's hall and she handed me a pink hospital bin of shower stuff, towel folded neatly on top of it.

"You can shower in there," she pointed to an open door. I looked in before slowly walking into the floor-to-ceiling cream-colored tiled room. Two pale green shower curtains hung on each side of the room and a drain was in the middle of the floor.

I opened the curtain furthest from the door and set my pink bin on the small tile bench in the wet shower space. I wasn't sure where to put my clothes to keep them dry. Hanging them over the shower rod with the towel seemed best. I shivered as I turned on the shower, making sure I faced the curtain, in case someone looked in.

When I was done showering and dressing in the clothes I'd worn in, I walked out the open door to find

Melanie sitting in a chair, a small desk in front of her with a stack of folders. She was writing in one.

She stopped and gave me a half smile. "Done?" she asked, reaching for my bin. She checked the items and tossed my wet towel in a laundry cart. Melanie paused, then pointedly asked, "Are you wearing that today?"

I raised my shoulders then let them drop and said, "I'll change in my room."

With that, she placed my bin on a two-shelved metal cart and rolled it into the nurse's station. Then she closed and locked the door behind her and led me back to my room.

I heard a knock on my door and then it slid open. Tara peeked in and glanced around our room like she was making sure I was alone. Another girl was with her—taller with long, dark hair and chestnut-brown eyes that flowed with her tanned skin. The tall girl flashed me a smile and plopped on the chair next to Tara's bed. Suddenly, Tara pulled a slice of bread out from under her shirt and her friend pulled out a Jell-O cup.

"This is all we could get from the lunch trays," the dark-haired girl whispered. "Anymore and they would've noticed." I hesitated, not sure if I should trust them. My hunger won out.

They laughed as they told me about the rumors going on outside our little room.

"The theory is, Dr. Sue has you on suicide watch. Don't worry; I set them straight," Tara said.

I stared at my feet again. "Thanks."

"Sure. By the way, this is Jessica. Hey, free time is almost over. We'll be back after group therapy."

I bit my lip to stop a grin from taking over my face. Apparently, when I stood up to Melanie about not drawing my blood that morning, I made some friends.

That afternoon, Melanie escorted me to Dr. Sue's office. I looked around the little room where there was nothing but a couch and chair in the room, with a painting behind the chair, and a small window. Dr. Sue walked in and sat down in the chair as Melanie closed the door.

"Take a seat," she instructed, so I teetered on the edge of the couch. I let Dr. Sue know I had read the rulebook, and I would not be taking meds or getting blood drawn. I hated needles like a cat hates water.

"Sam, we need to get blood from you to see what's going on in your body," Dr. Sue explained, not willing to give in either. "We're only allotted an hour session, so let's make the most of it."

Phew! I thought, not big at talking about myself. *Not sure what the point is of talking about things. People knew Logan and I needed help. The routine was that they would take us to a foster home, leave us for a week while Stacy would take some parenting classes and then they'd bring us back to her ... until it happened again.*

"Hello. Sam? You still with me?" Dr. Sue asked and I plopped deeper onto the red couch, sitting cross-legged, arms wrapped tightly across my chest while she read my folder. Without looking up, Dr. Sue asked how I felt about being there. I rolled my eyes. *Stupid question!*

She locked her eyes on mine, crossed her legs and wiggled her dangling foot. "Sam, did your mom hit you often?"

I looked at the picture behind her: a cabin next to a lake.

This room is hot. Wish that timer would go off so I could leave.

"Samantha, your mom told the caseworker that you're evil. That you have powers, like a witch. How do you feel about her saying that?"

I just studied the cabin. When Stacy would get us back, she would be fine for a month-ish, then it would start again. She would pack us up and move us as far as a tank of gas would take her. This went on until she met up with my two sisters' dad. I remember that day like it was yesterday.

What is she writing?

"Sam, do you believe you're evil?"

Can we open that window for some air? I bet it doesn't even open. Jeez!

She kept taking notes and tossing questions at me. Unanswered questions. For me, unanswerable questions. Towards the end of the hour, her voice became strained. Still calm but strained. I knew she was trying to understand and I also knew my silence was frustrating her.

The bell rang and I stood up. Before I left her office, she asked, "Is there anything you would be willing to trade for having the bloodwork done?"

I stopped. Scowled. "I wanna leave."

"Sorry, that won't happen."

I took a deep breath. "I've taken care of my sisters since they were born. Last night was our first night apart and I need to know they're okay."

She smiled. "If I can get your mom on the phone to see how the girls ... your sisters ... are, will you let us take your blood tomorrow morning?"

I hesitated. Finally, I whispered, "Yes," and walked out.

Tara appeared at my side. "How'd it go?"

I shrugged. "Okay."

"Good. You gotta come with me now; we're in the same group," she offered. We walked into the sitting room where all the teens gathered before splitting into two groups for our pre-dinner activity.

There were ten of us: six girls and the rest boys. The TV area looked different. The couches had been grouped to form a square so that we were all facing each other. A few adults walked in as Tara and I sat down next to Jessica.

"Good morning, everyone." A lady in pink scrubs pulled up a chair and sat down. "Two new family members joined us yesterday." Pointing at me, she said, "This is Samantha."

"Sam," I corrected.

She nodded and repeated, "Sam."

Then she pointed to a dark-haired guy sitting across from us. "And this is Eddy. Let's introduce ourselves. I'll start. Welcome, Sam and Eddy. I'm Debbie, the activities director."

I bet Eddy wants to be here as much as I do.

The group sat and talked for 45 minutes, leaving me out, to my relief. Debbie reminded us that we would have a movie Friday night and asked what we would like her to rent. After we picked *Drop Dead Fred*, she passed out our schedule for the week then sent us on our way.

Group B was written next to my name on the top of the paper she gave me. Tara and I glanced at each other's and I followed her to art. As I look back, it wasn't until Eddy stood up that I noticed how tall he was. He was wearing a black T-shirt and baggy jeans. He looked in our direction, and the dark shirt made his green eyes pop. But he wasn't heading in the same direction as Tara, which meant he was in Group A.

Bummer.

Our schedule was the same every day: Up at 6:30. Timed, eight-minute showers; a second over and the water would shut off. Breakfast at 7:00. Morning meeting at 7:30, followed by 15 minutes of free time.

Group A had class and then art one day and music the next, Group B had art or music, and then class. After lunch at 12:30, we met privately with our therapists three days a week. The other two days, we had group therapy. Then, an hour of free time until dinner at 6:00.

After dinner we were free until the lights-out meeting, where we talked about our day and recited the Serenity Prayer. In our rooms by 9:00, with lights out by 10. Thursday and Saturday nights were for parent visitation. Friday was reward day.

By the end of the week, I knew why Tara and I were roommates and had ended up in the same group. We were the only ones who never had a visitor. Never even a phone call.

We were both alone.

Chapter 2

Today, I had been here a week, keeping my head down and my mouth shut. When I was called to the staff station, I was nervous. You weren't called to the staff station unless you were in trouble.

What had I done?

Melanie's smile calmed my fear. "I just talked to Dr. Sue. She doesn't come in today, but she talked to your sisters' new caseworker who says they're fine. Someone's helping your mom with them."

"Oh, yeah? Does she know Mary can't sleep without a nightlight? And that Jackie's favorite bedtime story is *Goodnight, Moon*?" I was relieved that they were okay, but the idea of someone other than me taking care of them crushed me.

"... and Dr. Sue got your older brother's phone number."

I whispered, "Logan?"

"Yes. You can call and talk to him for 15 minutes. After we draw your blood tomorrow morning."

I walked back to Tara and sat on the floor.

Do my sisters miss me? Are they scared?

My mom was pregnant with me and living on the street when she met Logan's dad in a gas station. He was a widower, overwhelmed with the responsibility of a one-year-old son. He needed someone to care for Logan, and she needed a place to live, so they got married.

I thought about all the times Logan and I hid in the hall closet, afraid to move until my mother fell asleep. The times Logan's dad had "friends" over, and we were expected to disappear. They were big scary men who drove up on loud motorcycles. As soon as we heard the roar of their bikes, I'd find my plastic Breyer horse, Logan would grab a comic book or action figure, and we'd head under the porch steps to play in the cubbyhole we'd made under it. Blankets and snacks were hidden, waiting for us.

We kept each other safe. Until he left eight months ago, when he couldn't take it anymore. Logan's plan was to find a place out of state and get a job. I couldn't leave the girls; we both knew that. As he climbed out our window, Logan looked back and promised to return for us.

I hadn't heard from him since.

I looked around to see if anyone had noticed my conversation with Melanie. If they had, they didn't care. They were all playing pool or watching TV except for Tara. The way she was looking at me made me wonder if I was making weird faces.

"Did ya hear, Melanie?" I asked. She shook her head. "Dr. Sue has my brother's number. I can talk to Logan after I let them take blood."

"You have a brother? I didn't know you had a brother," she said curiously. "What about your sisters?"

"My sisters are okay, I guess someone is helping Stacy take care of them."

We leaned against the wall, pretending to watch the guys play pool.

I jumped when Tara announced, "Sam and I play the winners."

"I don't know how to play," I said shyly.

"Who cares. It's something to do."

Eddy appeared out of the TV area and came over to me. "I'll teach you," he offered quietly.

"What?" I asked, thinking I was hearing things.

"I'll show you. I know how to play. A little." He gave me a half smile.

"Nothing good on TV?" his roommate teased as he walked past us to take his last shot. The ball bounced off the side and missed the pocket.

"So do you want me to show you or not?"

I shrugged. "Sure."

Eddy was better at pool than he let on. I never got a turn.

"What's so funny?" I asked as I climbed into bed.

"Your face when Eddy offered to help you," Tara answered giggling. "You looked shocked."

"I was shocked," I mumbled. "Hey. How do we get clean clothes around here?" I had been washing the clothes I wore each day in our bathroom sink before bed.

"I'll show ya tomorrow. But you need a full load or they won't let you use the washer."

"Well, that stinks."

"I have some shirts you can add. We can ask if anybody else has anything to add to our load, but most parents take dirty clothes home on family therapy night."

"Hmm ... Tara? How did you end up here?"

She swallowed hard. "My mom remarried. Her new husband isn't nice. Actually, he's mean as hell to her ... and to me. He doesn't hit, but ... I don't know ... he's just not nice. He puts people down. She loves him and puts up with it. Puts him before me. It was too much. So, well, I tried to kill myself. My doctor says I'm bipolar. Maybe she's right."

I listened to her talk for a long time. When she was finally silent, I thought of the day Stacy met a man named Derek. (Logan's dad must have been gone now around a year.)

We had just moved into this new apartment. Stacy had been asleep for a few days and we were hungry. We were tired of PB&J sandwiches and found a box of mac-n-cheese in the cupboard. This apartment had a different stove, with a flame instead of hot coils. We had that flame too high and the next thing we knew, the apartment was full of smoke and firemen were at the door.

Logan let them in, and once they decided all was safe and the alarm was just due to the smoke, one of the firemen, Derek, sat with Stacy to write the report.

"So, Sam, you're nine, correct? And Logan you're 10?" They were married nine months later. Derek was her knight in shining armor.

Ours, too.

The first time someone asked if Mosquito Man had stabbed me yet, I asked, "Who?" Apparently, that's what they called the guy who sometimes took blood around here. The next morning, Nurse Steve woke me up before the sun could. Melanie held my arm tightly, and I tried not to pass out. Maybe it was the needle in my arm, the sight of the blood filling up that clear tube or maybe it was Melanie's firm grip.

I have to talk to Logan. I can do this.

When they left the room, I laid quietly trying to go back to sleep, but my arm was hurting where she had gripped it. The memory of the last time I had a needle in my arm made me wish I was asleep.

I was eight and since Logan's dad stopped coming home, his grandma would check in on us, bringing us food and toys. Once she brought us new shoes. When we asked her where Logan's dad went, she only smiled softly and said, "He's not coming back."

When she got to us this time, we looked like hell, Stacy had been gone for so long that we'd lost track of what day it was. Logan's grandma took us to the hospital.

I'd never forget the months leading up to that. My mom had taken me to a church where they all chanted my name and splashed water on me. When we got home, she locked me in my room, only letting me drink something that tasted horrible and smelled like Windex. She said it would get rid of the demon inside me. I was so thirsty, I drank it.

Logan snuck me food and water until he got caught, and then we were both in trouble. She locked the door and left. We were thin and hungry and weak. The whites of my eyes were yellow, and my fingernails were starting to fall out. Every time the nurse tried to put in an IV, my vein rolled or collapsed. She finally got it on my foot. We spent a few days in the hospital, but Stacy didn't come to see us. After we left the hospital, we stayed at Logan's grandma's house for a few weeks.

It was so nice at her house! She read us books and we baked cookies. But then Stacy came and took us home. A week later, the car was loaded and we drove all night. We never saw Grandma or school again.

I thought about my sisters.

Does Mom even realize they're there? Is she feeding them?

During the morning meeting, Debbie gave us the day's schedule and reminded us that family visitation was after dinner. Melanie said I could call Logan after group therapy. I couldn't wait!

First things first. I needed to do laundry. Tara and I asked around and gathered enough dirty clothes to start a load.

"What are you going to wear while yours are in the wash?" Jessica asked.

I shrugged. Even though the rulebook stated we couldn't share clothes, Tara offered me a pair of sweatpants. We figured since she only wore them to bed, the staff wouldn't notice. I still needed a top, one big enough to hide the fact that I wasn't wearing a bra.

I'll figure it out later.

When we turned to leave, I bumped into Eddy. He handed me a shirt. "I heard you talking this morning. You need a shirt? It's clean, but I need this back before my mom gets here tonight."

I reached for it, careful not to touch his hand.

"It matches your eyes," he added before walking away.

"He's weird," Jessica pronounced.

I just shrugged my shoulders and ran to change so I could add my shirt to our load. Weird or not, Eddy was a nice guy. Kinda cute, too.

We went through our normal morning schedule. During the first break, I moved the wet clothes from washer to dryer. As soon as the laundry was dry, I took it to our room, where I sorted and folded it before returning each item to its owner. I looked for Eddy and found him sitting in the dining room eating a snack with the other boys.

I scanned the room before walking in. Like every other room there, it had light-blue walls. There was no stove, I guess so we couldn't burn *this* place down. Next to the fridge was a table with stuff, like packets of ketchup and mustard. Across from it, a whiteboard with our schedule hung on the wall. In the center were six tables with four chairs each. A floor-to-ceiling window filled the far wall. It looked more like a meeting room than a kitchen or a dining room.

Crap, all the guys are there. I'll wait until he's alone. Oh, stop bein' a wuss, Sam!

I took a breath, walked over and slid his shirt across the table. He reached for it and our hands touched. For the first time, it didn't make me want to pull away.

"Thanks. You're a lifesaver," I whispered.

"Anytime," he answered. "Wanna snack?"

"Sure."

He pulled a chair over from another table. "Parent night tonight. Yours comin?"

Was he trying to be funny? Hadn't he noticed? No one comes to see me.

I swallowed hard. "No. I don't think so. Yours?"

"Yeah. My mom and dad."

I smiled and looked away.

Something about him is different. Eddy makes me ... nervous? No, not really nervous. Yet, nervous. Just a weird kind I've never felt before. Am I sick?

The guys talked about who was coming to visit them. The one sitting next to Eddy had dark, shaggy hair that covered one eye. I wondered why it didn't make him crazy. I wanted to reach over and shove it out of his face.

"This is Matt, my roommate." Eddy pushed Matt, who almost fell out of his chair. The guys all howled.

Matt kicked under the table at the kid across from him and said, "This is Tommy. He's in the room next to ours."

I know who they are. I've been here too.

"We've met. Hi, Tommy,"

He shot us an evil look. With his huge shoulders and tree-stump legs, he was like a football player. I learned this week that Tommy *hated* being called "Tommy."

"This is Jeff," Tommy said. Jeff seemed more interested in his magazine than us.

Matt was talking about how he hoped his brother would sneak him some smokes. He was dying for a hit and thought he'd found a way to smoke without getting caught.

"So, I'm going to stand on the toilet and blow smoke into the fan and the fan will suck the smoke out. They'll never smell it."

The image of him standing on the toilet, blowing smoke into the air vent had us all roaring till our faces hurt.

Once the laughter died down and the guys started talking again, I began to feel out of place.

I need to go find Melanie. Maybe I can Logan now.

"Tara and Jessica are probably looking for me," I said, getting up.

Laughing, Eddy pointed out the door. "Doubt it."

There were my friends holding up the wall, hands flinging and mouths going a mile a minute. I made my escape, nonetheless.

During class, Tara passed me a note. "Eddy is cute!" is all it said. I blushed and looked around the classroom.

The tables and chairs formed a U facing the teacher's desk. All the teacher did was hand out worksheets and then sit at her desk and read. When Mrs. Herzog handed me my assignment, she remarked, "We can't find any records for you after the third grade, so I don't know what level you're at, Sam. Try this."

I started the worksheet she gave me; math was not my best subject. My mind started to wander.

She pulled everyone else's papers out of big envelopes, but she got mine out of her desk. Maybe those are the envelopes parents trade with the staff on visitation night. Teachers are sending work in and parents are taking completed assignments back. No wonder I don't have an envelope; I don't have a teacher to send work or a parent to bring it in.

I tried to chop away at the worksheet until the hour was up. When I left class, a small, blonde girl stopped me.

"Hi, I'm Alice." She giggled like a hyperactive hyena.

"Hey. How are you?" I replied politely, trying to sound friendly, but I really just wanted to go find my friends.

Alice yacked on and on as we walked past the pool table into the TV area. I couldn't have gotten a word in if I'd wanted to.

Does she ever stop talking to breathe?

When we passed Tara and Jessica, they completely ignored us.

"My mom's gonna pick me up soon. I've changed my ways. I won't cause trouble anymore,'" she rambled.

I thought I was going to scream.

She got caught running away with her 25-year-old boyfriend. Big deal! My mom just threw me away. Oh, jeez, how can I be so rude? She has no clue about my life. How could she? And I won't talk about it.

"Dinner!" Someone yelled.

Finally, my chance to get away. "Talk to ya later." I sprinted towards the dining room to find Tara and Jessica. I sat down and rolled my eyes.

"You could have helped me."

"No way," they snickered.

"Well, you could have warned me."

They both shrugged and took another bite of their cheeseburgers. While we ate, they filled me in about Alice. Turned out, she annoyed everyone.

"Hey! Is that clock right?" I asked.

"What's with you and the clock tonight? You stretch your neck any more to see it, you're gonna turn into a giraffe," Jessica giggled.

"Families should be arriving soon."

"You're in a hurry for family therapy to start?" Tara raised her eyebrows. "What's Dr. Sue done to you?"

"Sheesh! I could care less about family therapy. When it's done, I get to call my brother."

I had barely gotten the words out when Melanie appeared at the doorway and announced that it was time to come to the meeting room.

The meeting room. Ha! It's the TV room unless parents are here.

Everyone was sitting with their families when we strolled in, and Jessica went over to hers. Tara and I asked almost in unison, "This is *family* therapy. Do we really need to be here?"

"Yes. You both know you're expected to be here whether you have family visiting or not," Melanie scolded.

The couches were full. Instead of pulling in chairs from the dining room, we sat on the floor against the back wall.

I had a clear view of Eddy. With a parent on either side of him, he looked like a kid in trouble. His mom was beautiful, tall and lean.

That's where he gets his looks. And he has her green eyes.

In her high-heeled shoes and flowered dress, she looked like she was going on a date. Her hair, perfect. Nails, perfect.

When the meeting started, I tried to pay attention, but I was bored. Parents were explaining why their kids were here and I really didn't care. I was more interested in Eddy's dad.

He was fidgeting, adjusting his striped tie and unbuttoning his dark suit coat. Then he checked his watch and whispered something to Eddy. They both nodded. His dad was nice looking, too. Tall, like Eddy. His brown hair was starting to gray, and he was clean-shaven.

I heard a wrapper crinkling and watched him pop some kind of hard candy into his mouth. When Eddy reached for one, his mom squeezed his knee and then glared around Eddy's back at his dad. Both of them straightened up in their seats and Eddy shoved his hands back into his hoodie pockets.

I stifled a laugh.

The parents were still talking about why they put their child into this place. Matt had his dad and brother,

Tommy had his mom, and Jessica had both parents. They were all in jeans and sweatshirts, so I wondered if Eddy's parents were going out to dinner later. Some of the teens were arguing their side of the story. I half-listened to Alice promise that she would not have sex with her boyfriends on her mom's bed anymore.

Finally, the families left for their teens' rooms. When the last parent walked out, I asked, "Can I call Logan now?"

Three big, black phones hung on the wall across from the pool table. Each phone had a slot to put in a coin, and a cord that connected the part you talk into to the part that you dial from. Each phone had a timer and required a code instead of money.

I waited for a staff member to unlock and dial the phone. Melanie pushed in a code, then set a timer, reminding me that I had only 15 minutes before handing me the talking end. A woman picked up.

"Is Logan there?"

"He's at work. Can I take a message?"

Noooo! Is this number even Logan's? Did they make this up to make me let them take my blood? Man, if it isn't a trick, I better be nice, or I'll never get to talk to him.

It took everything to collect myself. I quickly counted backwards from ten.

"Yes," I answered softly, "tell him Sam called. I'll call him back tomorrow." My throat was tight and my eyes burned. I held the phone in my hand for a few minutes, and when it started to beep, I hung up.

The voices of parents talking to their kids filled the hallway.

Head hanging and hands shoved in my pockets, I walked to my empty room.

Chapter 3

A few days later, I still hadn't talked to Logan. I decided I wasn't going to think about him. I couldn't. Melanie stopped me in the hall.

"I have some good news," she said. For a minute, I got my hopes up. As much as my life was hard at home, I missed my sisters.

Maybe my mom couldn't handle them and wants me back.

"Am I going home?" I asked, my voice a little shaky.

Melanie shook her head, but before I could react, she said, "Your brother called the staff station while you were in class. He works every evening, but he promised to call you Saturday around 7:00."

I nodded. "Okay. Thank you."

Saturday.

I needed to clear my head. Since it was free time and we weren't allowed in our rooms, I headed for the TV area, hoping to find an empty corner.

A few girls were carrying on in the dining room. Probably playing cards—War would be my guess. The boys were shooting pool and daring each other to annoy the staff tonight.

Alice and a new girl were watching *Doogie Howser, M.D.* I sat as far away as I could and pretended to watch it too. Alice was talking a mile a minute and I watched as the new girl's black-spiral hair bobbed up and down.

What did my sisters have for lunch? Did anyone hug Mary today? Mary loves hugs; Jackie just wants to sit next to you. Stop Sam! Just stop! There is nothing you

*can do about this so focus on doing what you have to so
you can get outta here.*

I automatically stiffened when Eddy suddenly sat next
to me. "Are you okay?" Can I sit next to you?"

"Sure. Is your game over?" I asked. I turned my head
and swiped my eyes with the sleeve of my shirt so he
wouldn't see that I'd been crying.

"No. You look upset, so I ducked out to check on you."

"I'm good."

"Are you sure you're okay?"

"I'm fine. You should go finish your game."

His eyebrow practically raised to his hairline.

"I'd rather sit with you, but we don't have to talk. I'll
just watch ... oh, perfect! *Doogie.*" He rolled his eyes and
put his hand on mine, I stiffened and the hair on my neck
raised. Eddy leaned back to stare at the TV.

Seriously! I just need a minute.

After a few minutes, my body relaxed, and I was glad
he was there. I actually felt comfortable and, somehow,
better.

"Sam. Sam. They're here! We have to go hide." Logan
woke me and I jumped out of bed. We started towards our
door but stopped. Heavy footsteps were on the stairs. We
looked at each other and climbed under my bed, pulling
the pile of clothes to cover where we'd climbed in. Logan
and I shoved our bodies against the cold hard wall. Lying
head-to-head, he grabbed my hand. The door flung open,
and the hall light shined around the front of the bed. We
held our breath.

Suddenly, a loud banging woke me up. I glanced at the
clock. Two a.m. I wiped the sweat off my face and laid still.
A staff member flung open our room door, walked in,
backed out, then closed the door behind him.

"They did it. I can't believe it!" Tara whispered.

"What? Who did what?"

"Shhh, don't let them know we're awake." With the second bang, she rolled over, giggling.

Did this have something to do with the way Eddy said goodnight? It wasn't so much *what* he said: "Try to sleep well." It was more *how* he said it. The stupid, smirking look along with the little-boy I-have-a-secret tone to his voice.

Two minutes later: Bang! from a different direction. The staff was running around opening and closing doors. *Bang!* Then *Bang!* Tara was doing her best to hold in a laugh. I tried not to move when our door opened again. "I know you're both awake," a male voice stated. We just held still.

He left our door open this time. The heavy click of the main doors made Tara and I look at each other. Keys clinking together filled the unit.

Uh, oh. They must have called for backup. This can't be good.

Metal folding chairs slammed open and we could hear adults talking. The frustrated staff seemed to be trying to figure out what was going on and how to stop it. Their sharp voices made me feel cold suddenly.

"One of us has to find out what's going on," Tara whispered.

"Do you want to peek out the door or should I?" I whispered back.

"Not me!"

"Fine, you sissy."

I cautiously tiptoed to the door and slowly edged one eye around the frame. Both of the night staff and three security guards were sitting cross-armed in chairs placed strategically around the unit, all our doors wide open. One guard was looking in our direction. I bolted back to bed and leapt under the covers.

Game over! We finally fell asleep.

At breakfast, smiles were plastered on the guys' faces until Melanie stormed in and demanded answers. Everyone stayed silent. Melanie stood firm as she let us know that "if anything like that happens again, you will all lose outside time for a week!"

Outside time? I can't lose outside time!

I'd been waiting to earn outside time, and today was the day I'd finally feel the sun on my skin.

Everyone was staring at their feet while Melanie took a deep breath and sternly told us, "We're in charge. The *adults* are in charge here ... by law, I can't lock you in your rooms for the day, but this will *never* happen again." Melanie stormed out of the room and we all busted into laughter.

"Figure it out yet?" Eddy asked.

"No." I hated feeling left out. I wish he'd quit trying to be clever and just tell me.

After what felt like for*ever*, he looked around then said quietly, "We put our shoes in our pillowcases, stood back and whacked them hard against the bulletproof window in our rooms."

Matt grinned, adding, "No matter how hard you hit them, they won't break. But they sound like a bomb exploding."

"And whose idea was that?" I asked.

"Mine, of course," said Matt smugly. "I read once that nothing breaks bulletproof windows."

"Well, aren't you clever." I exclaimed, holding back a smirk.

"Why, yes I am." He winked at me and picked up his toast.

"We had them running! Boy those windows were shaking," Tommy chimed in.

"Yeah, they still have no clue what the noise was," Matt said.

They chuckled.

I had to blink a few times for my eyes to adjust to the bright sunlight. All the windows were tinted and it took a minute to remember what sunlight was like. Eddy and Tommy looked small leaning against the seven-foot brick wall that framed our outdoor area.

Caged. Like animals.

Tara and Jessica were sitting at one of the ten tables that surrounded a volleyball court. Jeff was lying on the concrete slab that ran from wall to building, leafing through his surf magazine. He didn't seem to care if anyone else was around. Alice and Shannon were putting up a volleyball net. I took a deep breath and got the smell of warm concrete and fresh air. The only plants were potted bushes in each of the four corners. No flowers.

Matt was running from table to table looking for cigarette butts. "Matt, they emptied the ashtrays before we came out." Eddy shook his head and laughed.

"Screw you! I'm desperate," Matt snapped, checking the bushes next.

I joined Tara and Jessica. Jessica pulled out a deck of cards. "You in?"

I nodded, but before she had a chance to deal, Mike, one of the staff, yelled, "Okay. Everyone come here."

None of us were willing to lose outside time, so we gathered quickly. But when Mike divided us into two teams, we all groaned.

"Can't we just sit and enjoy the sun?" Jessica asked.

"No. We're playing volleyball, then a game of Trust."

"Great," I grumbled.

I was not much of an athlete, but I tried. I held my own, actually hitting the ball a few times. I loved being outside.

After volleyball, we grabbed cold drinks and sat on the warm concrete to listen to Mike explain how the Trust game worked.

"I am going to divide you into twos and blindfold one of you. The one blindfolded will fall back into your partner's arms. You're going to have to trust your partner to catch you. Then you'll switch roles. Volunteers?"

My palms started to sweat.

No way! I am not falling on someone! Is he insane? I jumped up.

"Can I use the restroom?"

Mike laughed. "I see we have a volunteer. Need one more."

Crap! No!

Eddy's voice broke into my thoughts. "I'll volunteer."

No way. He'll let me fall. I am not doing this.

I stared at Mike, acting like I didn't hear Eddy. "Mike, I don't want to play this game. And there's no way I can catch *him*."

Mike looked at me for a minute, then shook his head. "You can do this Samantha. Let's get started."

The others picked partners. Mike tied a blindfold on Jessica and then Matt. When he stood behind me, I pulled away, trying not to let his skin touch mine. The stiff fabric pressed over my eyes and then tugged on my temples. *Woosh.* Mike pulled the knot tight and walked away, his footsteps landing with a steady thud. Seeing nothing but dark fabric, I felt like vomiting and tried to peek under the blindfold.

Suddenly there were hands on my shoulders. Eddy bent over me and whispered, "Don't cheat." Then he turned my body so that my back was to him.

"This is not normal," I protested. "People don't fall on purpose. It's stupid!"

Eddy snorted. "How tall are you?"

I felt so short standing blindfolded next to Eddy, who had to be well over six feet. I wanted to run. "I'm five-one with shoes on. Shut up."

He bent so close that his breath warmed my ear. I stiffened.

"Trust me. I won't let you fall ... Shorty."

"Yeah, right."

Eddy laughed.

Mike said, "Okay. Ready? On the count of three, fall. One ..."

He can count all day. I'm not fallin'.

"Two ..."

No way!

"Three!"

I was a statue.

Now Eddy's breath was hot on my neck. "Come on. You won't get hurt."

I shook my head.

"I'll push her," Tara offered. "Are you ready to catch her?"

What?

Before Tara had a chance to lay her hands on me, I fell back. Everything went empty, hollow. Then, *wham!* Eddy's arms wrapped around me.

"I told you I'd catch you. You can trust me," he whispered.

"Your turn, smart-ass." I yanked the blindfold off my eyes.

"Um, I should have thought more about this. I mean, I'm way bigger than you," Eddy huffed, turning his back to me as Mike started the countdown.

I can't catch him. This is dumb.

Eddy stepped back in a pretending-to-fall action. I put my hand on his back as though I was catching him. We both laughed.

That wasn't so bad.

After the Trust game, Mike let us sit outside for ten minutes. Tara, Matt, Eddy and I sat at a table near the corner. Tara pulled out a deck of cards and asked, "Who's in?"

Matt grumbled something about needing a cigarette, then asked Eddy and Tommy to toss him over the wall before any staff returned. They just laughed.

Too soon, our time outside was up.

Back inside we all grabbed a juice box. Time to get to therapy sessions or class. I met with Dr. Sue, who wanted to know about my mother. As usual, I was vague.

"Sam, you do realize that you can't be placed until we resolve some of these issues, right? Tell me one thing. Just one thing. Like, how did you get your name?"

I shrugged. "Placed where?"

"A foster home, of course." Dr. Sue lowered her head and peered at me over the top of her glasses. "Unless you have any family we can call. Sam?"

"No." I looked out the window.

My brother, but he's a runaway.

"Your mother told us you are 'surrounded by evil'."

I was silent.

"It would help if you can you tell me anything about yourself. Okay ... How did Stacy pick your name?"

I sighed. "When they asked my mom what she was going to name her baby, she looked at the nurse who was holding me. Her nametag said *Samantha.* I heard my mom telling Logan's dad when he signed us up for school one year," I said robotically in a hushed voice. My eyes were focused on the cabin above Dr. Sue. The little rowboat tied to the dock.

"Hmmm. Thank you for sharing. Samantha is a pretty name."

I could feel her staring at me, waiting for more. When it didn't come, she said, "You can go to dinner now, dear." I got up to leave, but she continued. "Please think about talking to me. You'll feel better."

"I feel fine. Really." I straightened my back and lifted my chin.

I closed the door as I left and leaned against the wall.

When I was young, the social worker Darlene would visit our house. A lot. Each time—while she looked through the fridge and cupboards—she'd ask us how long Logan's dad had been gone. Before leaving, she'd pop her head in my mom's room and say, "Remember, I'll be back next week to check on these kids."

Occasionally, Darlene took us with her, giving us time to gather one set of clothes and what she called a "hug" item, some kind of stuffed toy or pillow. The first time, she wrote a note to Logan's dad and stuck it on the fridge. After that, she just tossed a business card on the table.

Sitting in her office for hours was not the worst part. It wasn't listening to her call foster homes or hearing her plead, "It will only be for a few nights. Just until we locate their dad." It was driving up to a stranger's house, walking to the door, holding each other's shaking hands, our free hand gripping our "hug," the fear of the unknown making our eyes swell.

We only let that happen a few times. We learned to tell whoever came to check on us that everything was fine. We learned to tell them Logan's dad was at work, even though he was gone. We got good at cleaning and making meals. We even learned to walk to the store and steal food. We learned.

Carefree laughter from the dining room snapped me back. Of course they could laugh; when their issues were resolved, they would go home to the parents who sent them here.

Only Tara knew that I had no home.

My friends were already eating. I sat next to Eddy and played with my food, pushing it from one side of my plate to the other and back again. Tommy reached over and took some of my fries.

"Aren't you hungry, Shorty?"

I flashed a fake smile. "Not really."

With that, three hands were on my tray and the food was gone.

Well, they left me a juice box.

"How was therapy?" Tara slapped Tommy's hand as he went for one of her fries.

"Fine." I mumbled. But the words *foster home* and *evil* echoed in my head.

Matt walked in and rattled on about the staff searching his room and finding pot. When Eddy kicked him under the table, Matt assured him that he let them know that Eddy knew nothing about it.

At the lights-out meeting, they announced that urine samples would be collected before going to bed.

I fought back the desire to kill Matt.

Chapter 4

The Tuesday morning meeting was always short and sweet, leaving time for group therapy. Melanie and Debbie told us that anyone who tested positive would receive the same punishment as Matt: "Only leaving your room for therapy and school, for one week."

When the four therapists sat down, I stared at my hands.

They better not expect me to talk.

"Shall we get started? Can anyone tell me what you could have done differently to avoid being sent here?" Dr. Sue asked. Alice started, of course. She was going home today.

After being caught in bed with an older man, Alice hit her mom and left. A "Really, Alice?" attitude swept the room.

I let out a quiet "humph" and shook my head slowly. But I knew I needed to stop thinking about my future and be happy for Alice.

Alice had finally stopped talking. "Thank you for sharing with us Alice. Eddy? Sam? You both have had two weeks to adjust to being here. It's time for one of you to talk," Dr Sue prompted.

I sat quietly between Tara and Eddy. My palms started to sweat and my hands were trembling. I rubbed my knees, hoping to settle my hands. After a minute of silence, Eddy took his hand out of his sweatshirt pocket and raised it.

"I'm ready."

"Thanks," I whispered. He nudged me with his elbow.

"My life is good," he started. "I have a younger brother and live with both of my parents. They rarely argue. My dad works a lot but that's what it takes to have the lifestyle we have. Plus, he likes what he does; he's a doctor. My mom is a stay-at-home mom. My parents consider us her job. And she can be ... annoying. Always wants to know everything. 'Who are you going to be with? Where are you going? What will you be doing?'

"I'm here because I messed up, I guess. She was cleaning my room ..." he paused, suddenly embarrassed, and then continued, "and found, umm, pot, a pipe and some other stuff under my mattress."

"When I got home from school, she was at the kitchen table, crying. I said hi and bolted up the stairs. She had been crying a lot lately and I just figured it was her time of the month. When I went into my room and saw the crap on my bed, I knew I was busted, so I grabbed it and left."

"Why didn't you talk to your mom? Face the music, so to speak?" his therapist prodded.

"I was mad! Yeah, I messed up, but she had no reason to search my room. I was not acting out; my grades were good and I was always home by curfew."

"Okay." Dr. Sue scribbled something, then looked up. "And where did you go?"

Eddy took a deep breath and let it out quickly. "I was going to just go for a drive, but I was pretty mad, so I walked two doors down to see my friend. I figured I would cool off and then go back. We got carried away, and, well, we ended up taking his dad's Mercedes for a ride."

All eyes were on Eddy.

His story was way better than Alice's.

"We just started to drive. Music up loud—"

"Who was driving?" she interrupted.

"My friend."

"Where were you going?" Matt asked.

"We didn't think that far ahead, just knew we were driving. Kinda stupid, looking back now." He pursed his lips.

"We were gone four days, ended up in Washington State somewhere. Not sure where. But we were almost out of money and gas. Definitely out of other things. We pulled over to sleep in a rest area when the police spotted the out-of-state plates, ran them, and discovered the car was stolen. We never thought about his dad reporting it stolen," he added ruefully.

"So, you were arrested for stealing a car?" Alice asked.

"Well," Eddy waved his head from side to side. "No. Yeah. As soon as we realized that the police had run the plates and were getting out of their car, my friend threw his dad's car into reverse and ... hit the police car." He laughed, so we all did.

Eddy went on. "Then we were arrested and taken back to California. I was in handcuffs when I walked into the police station where our parents were waiting. My mom's eyes were," and now he rolled his eyes so hard his eyebrows touched his hairline, "red and swollen. My dad's face was flushed and stiff." He sighed.

"The judge sent me here instead of jail. It helped that I wasn't the driver and didn't have a record."

The room was quiet except for a few snickers. I looked at Dr. Sue, who was watching Eddy.

"See. You all have to understand my parents. My parents never hit us, but they taught us right from wrong. How to act. Manners. We go to church every Sunday, sick or not. They would hug us when we left the house and when we came back. I never missed a meal. My brother and I play any sport we want. Well, in our house, no sports on Sunday's. You know—we can't miss church. We have a nice house. They gave us everything we need or want. I knew better. They deserved better."

When he stopped talking, disappointment with himself burned in his eyes. I sympathy-bumped him with my shoulder; he bumped back.

Over the next few days, Eddy and I spent all our free time together. During the Thursday morning meeting, Melanie's face was bright when she announced that although some of us had slight traces of drugs in our systems, they were sure it was just lingering from before we got here. We wouldn't be punished.

For our outdoor time this week, we would take a supervised walk to the video store. Well, except Matt. He was still in trouble for the whole pot thing. The store was just around the corner, but we were excited at the chance to do something normal-ish.

That evening, Tara and I watched as the parents greeted their kids with hugs and kisses. I was surprised that no one seemed embarrassed.

We found a couch that wasn't occupied and sat facing the group. Eddy's parents were dressed up again.

"Feel outta place?" I whispered to Tara.

She groaned. "Yep."

The pot issue started the meeting with a bang. Matt's dad shook his head as the staff explained that they searched Matt's room and found pot and tin foil from our baked potatoes, even though it was hidden, taped underneath his dresser drawer. Matt's dad asked him what he was thinking, but Matt didn't answer.

Eddy's dad cleared his throat; his mom's face turned red and her eyes began to leak.

Eddy's voice was firm. "I did not touch it."

Matt confirmed Eddy's statement, but Eddy's dad's mouth went straight and his eyes got tight. He spoke calmly, but his words were clipped. "Edward. You are here because we found that green shit in your room. Do you expect me to believe that your roommate smoked it and you didn't?"

Silence.

"Why didn't you then, son?"

Eddy scowled. "Yes, Dad. That is exactly what I expect you to believe. I promised you I wouldn't. Plus, I didn't want to lose a week of free time."

They stared at each other down for a moment. Dr. Sue settled it by saying, "Urine tests were done on everyone. Eddy's been cleared."

His dad's face softened and he nodded once to his son.

"Good. But you are well aware of the doubt you've created. It will take time to earn that trust back."

"Yes, sir," Eddy snapped, like he was in the military. I stiffened, waiting for the arguing to begin again, but after a moment Eddy added, "Dad. It was a stupid mistake. I have too much to lose. I get it. I *won't* do it again."

His mom dried her eyes. Eddy looked at me and tried not to smile.

"Stop! Who are you? Only family can be in here!" Melanie barked suddenly. I turned to see who she was yelling at.

"I am all the family she's got," the guy at the doorway stated.

"Logan?"

My brother walked in the room. He looked ... different. Same dark hair and green eyes, but taller and thinner. I lunged toward him.

"Sam! Are you okay?" He pushed me arm's length away and looked me over. "Listen, I don't have much time. My ride isn't allowed in, and he'll only wait 15 minutes. Did anyone hurt you? I am so sorry. I didn't think it would take so long to get here."

I bit my lower lip to fight back a grin. "I'm fine. I'll go get my stuff."

He looked down at his feet.

"Logan? I don't have much. I'm ready to go," I assured him, taking a step back. He grabbed my arm, but didn't look at me.

"They won't let me take you," he whispered.

I straightened up. "What? Why?"

"I'm not old enough and that bi ... your *mother* gave you to the state. She signed papers and all."

"I know. I heard Darlene and Stacy talking about it. So?" I shrugged.

Logan stared hard at me. I had seen that look on his face once before, the night he climbed out of our window. Flat and hollow. I hated that look.

I forced a smile and asked, "A foster home? Or a group home? Those are my options. Right?"

He continued looking at me. His nostrils flared, and he took a deep breath, shaking his head as he slowly let the breath out.

"Then what? Back to her again? Did she have to take more classes?" I asked louder. Part of me wouldn't mind that. At least I'd know the girls would be okay.

"Sammie, you are too old. Darlene can't find a long-term foster home for you. I met with her this morning; she's helping me get emancipated. She's how I got in the front doors."

"Ohhhh. That's okay." I shrugged. "It's not too bad here."

"Sam. You're going to a detention center when you leave here. Juvie." He winced.

My eyes were hot, and my throat stung. I tried to shut off my emotions. "A detention center? That can't be too bad. Right? Logan?" I choked over my words.

He whispered, "You seem safe here. As soon as you leave here, I'll come for you. We *will* run. You will not sleep one night in a detention center. I can't even think about it"

"Can't be that bad. Don't worry, Logan. If I was able to survive Mom, then I can survive this." I gave him a teasing punch in the shoulder, but his worried face was making it hard to stop my tears and I needed to stay strong.

I saw his lip try to curl into a smile. "Oh, Sammie. No, this is different. Mom didn't break your spirit. But I'm afraid this will. My buddy just turned 18 and got out of one. "

Darlene interrupted. "Five minutes. I'll tell your friend you're coming."

Logan didn't shift his eyes away from me but nodded.

"Are you coming back?" I asked, feeling the burn in my eyes creep down my cheeks.

"I want to, but my buddy and I both had to take the night off from work. It's a two-hour drive each way. I don't see how I can." He looked me over head-to-toe and rolled his eyes. "Is this all she let you take?"

"And one change of clothes. I make it work." I poked at the hole in my shirt. He pulled off his sweatshirt and his T-shirt. I could see his ribs and wondered if he was eating. Logan handed the warm Logan-scented clothes to me and put his coat on.

He bent close so only I could hear him. "Let me know when they're moving you. Stay strong. Remember street signs."

"Logan!" Darlene snapped. He spun away. I leaned as far as I could to watch him go out the main front door. His shoulders slumped and he walked like he was fighting the urge to look back.

"Can I go to my room?" I asked not turning around.

"No," Dr. Sue said. "We have work to do."

"You'll get nothing out of me tonight." My eyes were starting to swim. I wondered if I ran for my room, if anyone would stop me. Dr. Sue took a step toward me. I stiffened and pulled back. "Don't touch me," I growled, emphasizing *don't*.

"Sam? Let's talk about what just happened." Her voice was tender, like she was talking to a scared puppy.

Someone moved behind me and picked up my hand. I tried to jerk my hand away but couldn't.

"Go away."

"Maybe talking to us will help." Eddy said. It was him trying to hold my hand. I pulled my hand free.

Hot tears streamed down my cheeks. I hurried to wipe them away and mumbled, "Eddy—I *can't* let them see me cry."

"Crying isn't bad. It shows you're human."

"No. It shows that you're weak."

He cleared his throat. "Weak? Dr Sue? Can we have five minutes, please? Maybe she'll talk to Tara and me?"

She paused for a minute. "All right. But, Sam, you and I need to talk about this later. Stay in the kitchen."

I jerked forward, Eddy and Tara by my side.

As soon as we were in the kitchen, he pulled me into him. I tensed up and tried to push him away, but he held tight, and I gave in, I couldn't stop the tears. They wouldn't stop! Tara put her hand on my back and said, "I know. This sucks, Sam."

After a minute, I pulled away and Eddy let me. Tara, Eddy and I sat down at the closest table.

"How does crying make you human? It makes me feel stupid," I sniffed, wiping my eyes with a napkin.

He picked strands of hair off my wet cheeks. "Are you ready to go back?"

"No!" I must have sounded like a little kid who'd been asked if she wanted to eat her broccoli.

He gave me a half-laugh and kissed my forehead. "You don't have to be so tough."

"Nobody wants me. Any hope I had of surviving just walked out that door. I *have* to be tough."

"You're okay for now, and you have me."

"Us," Tara corrected.

"Oh. Well, then," I mocked.

"Melanie's watching. We need to get back in there," he said. The room was silent when we took our seats. I half listened to the rest of family therapy. When it was over and parents went with their kids to their rooms, I got up to walk to mine, but Dr. Sue stopped me with a commanding, though soft-spoken, "Let's have a chat."

I sat with her and listened to her explain that she would do all she could to help me, but my mind was running faster than a racehorse as reality set in.

She really left me here. She's not coming back. And no one can do anything about it—not even Logan.

Chapter 5

Melanie snapped ID bands onto our wrists and said, "Okay. Remember, this is a reward. If any of you leave the group, you will not see the light of day for weeks."

Melanie, Mike, and six more of us headed toward the video store. Eddy grabbed my hand, and I looked to make sure Tara was next to me. We were smiling like a group of kids at Disneyland.

As we passed street signs, I repeated the names and directions in my head. *Left on Madison, right on Fifth.* The slight breeze rustled the leaves on the trees and felt refreshing on my face.

Each of us tugged at our sweatshirts to pull the sleeves over the gray hospital-style ID bands. I was wearing Logan's sweatshirt, which was way too big and hung down to my knees. There was a chill in the air and I was glad I had it.

The video store had opened a half hour early so we could pick a movie before other customers arrived. An old, gray-haired guy unlocked the door. Once we were all inside, he relocked it and introduced himself as Henry, the store owner.

The small store smelled like a stale dusty attic. Henry's back was humped and his whole body trembled as he gave us a brief tour. I wondered if we made him nervous or if he was shaky because of his age.

Video cases filled the shelves that lined the store. Two rows of shorter shelves ran down the center of the space. I picked up a movie and started to read the back. Eddy hugged me from behind. "If you're planning to run, today is not the day."

Tara tapped me with her elbow. "Not without me," she mumbled.

I simply nodded, looked around and sighed, "Jeez, I don't have my movie yet."

Eddy let me go and picked up an adventure movie. He read it quickly and moved on to another one.

Jeff was by himself, so I went to see what he was looking at. "What'd you find?" I asked. "*Point Break*," he said and pushed the surf movie in my direction. I read the back and told him it sounded interesting. I handed it back before returning to Eddy, Tara and Jessica.

"These cases are empty," I observed.

Eddy shook his head. "Each movie case has a number taped to it. It matches the number on the tag hanging below. See?" Eddy pointed to numbers highlighted in yellow on a tag. "The movies are behind the counter. Henry pulls them by the number on those tags."

"Oh. Have you been here before?"

"Nah. I heard Henry tell Mike."

Surprisingly, the six of us agreed on two movies in twenty minutes.

We shuffled back to the lockdown center. Melanie and Mike cut off our bands as we entered the building. The doors slammed shut. Click.

By the time the dinner cart was rolled into the dining room, we were ready to eat. Each tray had a name on it and slid into a slot, like at a hospital.

I was actually hungry and wolfed down the chicken breast, but as soon as I started to push my green beans around my plate, Tommy reached over the table and snatched my foil-wrapped potato.

"She might have wanted that," Eddy snapped.

We all looked at him. Tommy normally eats what I don't at dinner. Eddy eats my breakfast toast.

"She doesn't," Tommy said flatly. He opened a butter packet and squeezed the butter onto my not-so-warm potato.

"Just ask her next time. Jeez!" He picked up his plastic tray and slid it into the metal cart.

I handed Jeff my ice cream cup and put my tray away. "What's with you?" I asked Eddy when I reached the pool table. He was absentmindedly stacking the pool balls.

He handed me a stick, eyed up the table, and said, "You were actually eating for once." He broke the cluster and two balls went in. "I'm stripes." He gestured toward the solid red ball, which was sitting inches away from the middle pocket. "Think you can get that one in?"

Jessica came out of the dining room and challenged me to a game of War. I nodded, then looked over the table like I was a pool shark. I leaned over, lined up the shot and ... missed. Eddy snickered and I handed the stick to Tommy.

"Oh, come on. Don't be mad," Eddy urged.

"Pssh. I'm not mad. Just better at War."

Tara, Jessica and I sat in the dining room and started a three-person game with two decks of cards.

The boys were challenging each other, and their rowdy voices kept interrupting my concentration.

"Okay, let's play with our left hands only." Tommy suggested.

"Doesn't matter if they're solid or stripes," Jeff added.

Shannon popped her head into the dining room. "Movie time!" she announced.

We kept playing until the pre-movie commercials started. Jessica sat next to Shannon with her bowl of popcorn. Tara and I took our normal places on the floor against the back wall. Eddy sat next to me with his bowl of popcorn and a can of Coke.

"How's Matt holding up?" I whispered. He pointed down the hall. I leaned over and saw Matt sitting in the doorway of their room so he could watch the movie.

"As soon as the staff sees the door open, he'll be done. I snuck him some popcorn." He shoved his hand in his bowl and flipped popcorn into his mouth.

"Eddy?"

He slid an arm over my shoulders and pulled me close. I resisted pulling away.

"Hmm? Want some?" He set the popcorn bowl on my lap. I took a few kernels. He tried to hand me his can of Coke, but I shook my head. He took a swig.

"You were right. I was thinking about running today. At the video store."

"I know." He kissed the top of my head. "Will you do something for me?"

"Maybe. Depends on what you want," I teased.

"Will you let me know when you decide to go? I want to go with you."

I thought for a minute. "No. I can't ask you to do that. Logan will get me from wherever they send me," I said, trying to be quiet.

Tara nudged me. "This movie is getting good. Go talk somewhere else." I stood up and could feel Eddy's eyes following me as I left for the kitchen. After a minute, I heard his steps behind me.

I grabbed a snack, not really caring what it was. Eddy set his Coke and popcorn on the table and sat down. Mike poked his head in. "Everything okay here?"

"Yes. We're just not into the movie," Eddy answered. He pivoted the upright Coke can on the table.

Mike studied us for a minute. "Okay. Well, leave this door open," he instructed, tossing a deck of cards on the table as he left the kitchen.

Eddy picked up the deck and started to shuffle.

"Sam, can I ask you a question?"

"Sure. What's up?"

"Why did your mom sign you over to the state?" He started passing out cards.

I took a deep breath.

Do I really want to tell anyone what I have been through? No, not just anyone. But Eddy? Yeah. Maybe.

"It's a long, complicated story," I stalled, picking up my cards.

"I think I can keep up."

"Are you sure you want to know this?" I set the cards face down in a line to play Trash as he put his hand on mine.

"Please? I want to understand. My parents would never—"

"Fine. I'll tell you. But I would rather not."

"I really want to know."

"Jeez. Okay. Stacy never wanted me. She was young," I started.

"Then why did she have you? Just tell me." he flipped a card over and set one down.

"When Stacy was 15, she was raped. A few months later, she realized she was pregnant and tried to get an abortion at a free clinic. They told her she needed her parent's consent. She had told her parents about the rape after it happened, but they didn't believe her. From what I've heard, she was always seeing things and telling stories. When she told them she was pregnant, they kicked her out. They didn't want to be embarrassed by a pregnant teenage daughter."

I paused to look at his eyes to see if I could figure out what he was thinking. He flipped another card and set one down. I picked it up and placed it in order.

He gave me a half-smile and said, "Go on."

I took a deep breath and huffed it out. "A friend's mom let her stay with them for a few days and took her back to the clinic, but the doctor told my mom that the baby was too old to be aborted. Stacy told me over and over, she tried everything to get rid of me. Obviously, nothing worked. She lived on the street or at friend's houses for a while. Until she met Logan's dad."

When I finished telling the story, Eddy just shook his head. He finally asked, "So Logan isn't your brother?"

I hesitated. "Not by blood, no. But he is more my brother than Stacy is my mother."

"Okay."

"That's enough. Please don't tell anyone," I begged, starting to get up. Eddy grabbed my hand. "What happened to Logan's mom?"

I sat back down. "She overdosed after Logan was born."

"So, your mom tried to abort you, but it didn't work. So, she kept you and was mean to you? She didn't give you up for adoption? I don't get it."

"I told you, it's complicated," I said, starting to feel annoyed. "Yes, she kept me. But every time she looked at me, all she saw was her rapist's eyes." I stopped, wishing I had not told him about my eyes.

Eddy stared at me like he was trying to soak it all in. "Jeez, those eyes are what sucked me in."

I fidgeted. "I think my mom tried. I mean, she was so young. I think she thought it was the right thing to do, to keep me. But a forced baby. Then she met a guy, Logan's dad, a widow with a kid. So, a marriage deal. She was sixteen years old with two babies—had to be hard, you know? Plus ... Logan's dad wanted us." I gave him my "all is good" smile that Darlene had learned not to believe.

He scowled. "Was Logan's dad nice?"

"He was but he worked a lot. When I was eight, I think, he left for work one day and never came back. At first we didn't dare ask where he was. Then we saw a letter on the table. He was killed by a drunk driver. Stacy was overwhelmed. Each of us reminded her of men she didn't love. Trust me, she didn't have any trouble reminding us of that."

It was easy to talk to Eddy, but I decided he knew enough for now. Actually, more than I wanted him to know. I was relieved when he looked away for a second. Then he leaned over and gently kissed me.

Boy, was I confused!

We talked until the movie was over. He told me more about his family. It was a nice change to hear about him making cookies with his mom and the sports he played. "I've tried it all, but hockey is my favorite. The team I'm on now is heading toward playoffs."

I smiled at some of his stories and could tell that his parents never hurt him. *He is cute,* I kept thinking.

Matt came in announcing: "Sam. Eddy. Lights out in 15 minutes."

"Who let you out?" Eddy joked.

"They said I could get a drink before lights out," he answered, giving Eddy a playful punch on the shoulder and sitting down.

Tara came in with tear-filled eyes followed by Tommy, who handed her a can of Coke from the fridge. Tommy rolled his eyes and groaned, "What a stupid movie! We should have gotten *The Terminator*."

Matt and Eddy laughed.

"I picked this one out." Tara gave them all a look that clearly said, *"Shut up!"*

Much to my surprise, they did.

Chapter 6

"We'll have to escape after night shift starts. Once we're a few blocks away, we can call Logan to come get us," I told Tara, while getting ready for bed.

"Yeah, daylight staff watches us way too close," Tara agreed.

I had their schedules down to the minute. Monday through Wednesday, Melanie arrived for morning bed check and stayed until 3:00. Mike showed up by 2:30 and did the nightly bed check. On Thursday and Friday, they switched.

Caregivers hovered over us all day. They had to swipe a card to get in and out. The school, music and art teachers had to be signed in and out. Therapists too. The food crew rolled our cart of trays in at 6:45 am, 11:45 am and 6:45 pm every day. All doors were always locked, alarmed and watched.

But the night shift had two staff members, a male and a female. They arrived at lights out and left as the breakfast cart arrived. And I'd noticed that one caregiver dozed off around two in the morning and the other went out to smoke at midnight and four.

We could pull this off.

"Lights out!" Melanie yelled. The door creaked open at 10:02 and Melanie said, "Good night, ladies."

I smiled. *Right on time.*

When she clicked our door shut, I jumped up and carefully cracked it open so we could hear them.

"They're all in bed. See you Monday morning," Melanie told the night guy.

"Alright. Have a good weekend," he answered. We never got to know the night caregivers; they were only there if we needed something and to keep guard.

At 10:15 p.m. the door groaned open, a light ran over us and the door eased shut.

"We could go now," I whispered. "By 7:00 we'll be miles away."

"Okay, but how do we get out?" Tara whispered back.

Our door complained again and I froze.

Shit. The night guards heard me!

"Scoot over."

I turned and was face-to-face with Eddy.

"What are you doing? We're gonna get in trouble," I whispered, sliding to one side.

"I have it covered," he said with confidence.

I tensed up and pulled the blankets tight around me.

"Don't worry. Tommy has the staff looking for his inhaler. He can't remember if he left it in the boys' shower or the classroom."

"I didn't know Tommy had asthma."

Eddy grinned like a kid playing a trick on his teacher. "He doesn't. Jeez, your room is cold!"

"I have extra covers at my feet. Want them?"

He slid an arm around my shoulders, putting the other behind his head. "Nah, I'm good. Don't wanna get too comfy." He leaned forward and kissed my forehead.

I held my breath. My heart was racing so fast that I wondered if he could hear it.

"Breathe, Sam. We won't get caught. At about midnight, the guy disappears for a few minutes. We think he goes outside to smoke. Matt's going to fake a stomachache and ask the lady for meds."

I giggled and so did Tara. "You're still awake?" I mumbled to her.

"Not for long. Let's continue planning tomorrow night," Tara said. She discreetly put in her headphones and rolled over.

"When the lady goes into the backroom to get meds for him, I'm outta here. For now, though, we're alone." Glancing at Tara, Eddy added, "Well, almost."

"How long have you been planning this?" I asked, curling up against him.

"A few days. Matt and I started watching the night crew. Did you know there's only two of them?"

My face got hot. "A few days? Eddy? You can't run away with me."

"I know I can't. It's kinda fun to think about. I just wanted to see if I could actually sneak in here and back out."

He gave my neck a light kiss. It tickled. I scooted closer to him.

"I thought you were studying this place for a quick departure," Eddy said.

"I *am*. I was trying to figure out daylight loopholes, but I got sidetracked." He stifled a laugh. "The kitchen crew even checks the rolling cart."

"Hmmm. We could never run during the day, the way they're all over us," he said, and started kissing my neck, then across my jaw to my lips. I tensed up and the hair on my neck started to itch. Eddy felt my resistance and pulled away a little. After a few minutes that tense feeling left and my eyes got heavy.

Jennifer, the head weekend caregiver, opened our door and said, "Tara. Sam. Time to get up. You two going to shower?"

Panic raced through me.

Damn! We fell asleep.

I waited for her to say something to Eddy, but she just shut the door. I opened one eye and felt the other side of the bed.

Whew! He's gone.

Tara lifted her head, smiled at me and collapsed into laughter. We jumped up and bolted for the shower room.

Hot water!

"Sorry. You're the last ones, girls," Jennifer said, not sounding sorry. We groaned.

Tara was singing the Beatles' tune "Let It Be" while she showered. I flung my towel over the curtain rod, showered, shaved my legs and washed my hair in silence.

I didn't remember Eddy leaving our room. I could only hope he didn't get caught on his way back to his room.

While Jennifer checked my bin, I tapped my foot impatiently and glanced toward the dining room. "Everything looks good, Sam."

I nodded. I hated acting like a lovesick chick, but I couldn't help myself. I turned sharply and headed to the dining room. No Eddy. No Matt. Did they get caught?

Maybe they already ate and were watching TV. Nope. Jeff was alone, staring out the window. His back was to me, and the morning sun shone on his sun-bleached hair. It was the first time I'd noticed his surfer style, the baggy shorts, the wave on his T-shirt, flip-flops and dark tan.

I took a deep breath and went to see what he was looking at. Eddy and Matt?

"You okay, Jeff?" I asked.

He nodded. "Hey, Sam. It's a beautiful morning."

"Yeah, it is." The sun was peeking over the wall and the empty patio.

"I bet the beach is getting crowded," he mumbled.

"Yeah, it might be."

He smiled, leaning his face up to the sun and said, "God, I need outta here! I'm on dawn patrol."

"You miss the beach police?" I asked.

"No. Why would I? Oh. Yeah, I said dawn patrol. Sorry, What I mean is I miss surfing early in the morning. When the sun starts to come up and the air is crisp."

I stood next to him and soaked up the sunrays.

"Hey, you two, the cart leaves in ten minutes. Better eat," Jennifer called out.

"Yes, ma'am," Jeff answered.

Matt and Eddy walked into the dining room. They looked like they'd just crawled out of bed. I turned to go see them but felt rude.

"Jeff, did you eat?"

He didn't look away from the sunrise. Even though he always ate alone, I didn't feel right just ignoring him.

"Well, I'm going to eat with Matt and Eddy. You're welcome to join us," I added.

I grabbed my tray and sat next to Eddy. "You scared me! I thought you'd either left or gotten caught."

He leaned over, kissed the top of my head and grabbed my toast. "Nah. Best plans, huh? We really did oversleep. Hey, who's that you were talking to?"

"Where have you two been?" Shannon asked.

Matt rubbed his eyes and groaned, "We overslept."

Jeff walked in, grabbed his tray, and sat at the end of our table. Everyone stopped eating and stared. He never ate with us but preferred to sit by the window and look at his magazine.

"What?" he said.

The weekends were pretty much all free time unless a therapist came in or we needed to make up a class. The staff just kept an eye on us.

The Saturday morning meeting was short. Jennifer reminded us that parents would arrive at 11:00 and we had a music class to make up.

"Any questions?" Jennifer asked.

I cleared my throat and raised my hand.

Jennifer stopped, clearly surprised that I was willing to speak up. "Yes, Sam?"

"It's a nice day out."

"Yes, it is."

I hesitated, then asked, "Do you think we could visit families on the patio today?"

There was a long silence while Jennifer flipped through the papers on her clipboard. "I'll make a phone call and let you know."

Jennifer left when the music teacher arrived. "We're going to learn a few new songs today," Sandy said cheerfully.

She handed each of us a three-ring binder filled with sheets of song lyrics and we flipped through it while she got her guitar out. We sang along to *Under the Boardwalk* and *In My Life*. We asked her if she had any songs we knew. She sat back in her seat and gave a long sigh.

Throwing her hand on her heart, she exclaimed, "You *have* to learn these songs. They're great! Classics. Absolute classics!"

"Parents are here," Tommy announced, before tossing his pool stick on the table. Jeff gave his mom a hug. His dad shook his hand and handed him a new surf magazine.

Jessica giggled and told her mom that her mom's new haircut was cute.

Eddy greeted his mom with a tight hug and then reached over and grabbed the lady that had walked in with her. I did a doubletake. She looked just like his mom. Both women were stunning in their designer jeans, beautiful shirts and well-matched jewelry.

"Are they twins?" Tara asked me.

"Sure looks like it," I answered with a shoulder shrug.

"Ladies?" Jennifer said. She tilted her head toward the dining room, and we reluctantly followed her. She sat down and knocked on the table across from her. Tara and I looked at each other, then sat.

"I brought you two a new card game." She smiled and set a little red box on the table.

"Skip-Bo?" Tara and I asked together.

Jennifer explained the rules and said, "I'll play until you understand." Ten minutes later, she went back to work and we headed to our room, cards in hand.

A tap on the door interrupted our game.

"Yo!" Tara yelled. I rolled my eyes.

Jeff poked his head in. "Sam? Tara?"

"Hey, what's up?" I asked.

He fidgeted with the door handle and said, "Um. Jennifer talked to Mike. You can play your game outside." He turned and walked away. We looked at each other for a minute, then grabbed our cards and rushed out.

Families were crowded around the tables and the green umbrellas were popped open. We found a shady spot by the wall and sat on the concrete.

When Eddy walked over, we were deep into our game. Tara put down a card that messed me up, and I scowled for a moment. "Hmm. Take that!" I teased, slamming a card on top of hers. She stuck her tongue out at me.

Eddy knelt down, balancing on the balls of his feet.

"Yo!" I said, mimicking Tara.

"My mom and aunt asked me to invite you two to sit with us," he said.

"Why?" I grumbled.

He raised his eyebrows. "Come visit. Please? I'll play cards with you guys when they leave."

Eddy stood up and offered us each a hand. We grabbed on and he pulled us up and took us over to the beautiful maybe-twins.

"Mom, Aunt Tracy, this is Sam and Tara," he said.

"Hi," we said, almost together.

"It's nice to meet you both," his aunt offered.

I felt odd sitting with Eddy and his family, listening to them talk. I felt even more uncomfortable when his mom turned her attention to me.

"Sam? Edward told us that he cares greatly for you."

I bit my nails and gave a small nod. "Yes. We've become good friends.

I was wrong – Eddy doesn't have her eyes. His are much kinder.

"Where is your family, dear? I mean, besides your brother. Where are you from?"

I paused. I really didn't want to discuss my family with Eddy's mother. I swallowed hard and whispered, "San Diego."

"That's not far from here," she observed and looked at Eddy.

"No, it's not far at all," his aunt agreed. "And I must say, you both have perfect skin."

I looked at my hands. I had no idea what to say to that.

"Sorry, Sam. I didn't mean to embarrass you. I imagine, dear, you'd look even cuter if you cut off those split ends."

Eddy's eyes went wide then back to normal.

Split ends?

I wanted to crawl under the table. Thank God I was saved by Jennifer yelling for Tara, who didn't seem too pleased. Her head popped up toward the patio door, but she froze when she saw Jennifer walking toward us with a lady in tow who was wearing a large flowing muumuu.

"Tara," I whispered, "who is that?"

Tara didn't look away from the fall-flower attack heading our way. "My dad's sister, I think."

The gold bracelets on the lady's arm clattered when she shoved her hand toward her. "Hi, Tara, I'm your Aunt Tiffany. Remember me?"

Tara stood up and took Tiffany's hand. "Yes, I think you're the aunt from New Jersey. I've seen pictures of you at Dad's—your hair kinda stands out."

"Yes. Red and curly, just like yours." Her aunt smiled, still holding onto Tara's hand. When she finally let it go, she gave Tara's shoulders a light squeeze. "Glad to finally meet you. I'm living in San Francisco now, and as soon as I heard you were here, I contacted the Center."

With a whirl of motion, Darlene rushed through the patio door, arms piled with papers and interrupted them.

"Sorry I'm late. Tiffany, I'm Darlene. I am here to help today," She offered Tiffany her hand.

"Nice to meet you, Darlene. My brother told me you could help us figure this situation out," Tiffany smiled.

"Situation?" Tara whispered.

"Yes, let's go call him," Darlene said. She motioned for Tara to follow them.

Eddy's mom and aunt watched them leave and went back to chatting with Eddy. They talked about Eddy's brother and his cousin, Tracy's son, who was a year older than Eddy. I bobbed my foot, thankful to be off the hot seat. Eddy put his hand on my knee.

I wasn't really listening to them talk; I was wondering if Tara would need to run away tonight.

Chapter 7

Tara didn't talk much about her aunt's visit. When we asked her about it, she just changed the subject. Until after the last bed check, Sunday night.

"My dad called her; he wants me to go live with her," Tara said flatly.

I lifted my head off the pillow and asked, "Who? Your aunt?"

"Yeah, who else would I be talking about?"

"Why can't you go back to your mom's or live with your dad?"

"My mom said it's my dad's turn to deal with me, but he travels for work. He thought his sister and I might need each other."

"Oh. So, are you going to go live with her?"

"Don't think I am being given a choice. During our conference call, Darlene told my dad she would send him the necessary paperwork. Once it's signed, I'm going to San Francisco."

She picked up the earpieces from her CD player and untangled the two wires.

"Is she nice? I mean, do you like her?" I asked. She stopped fiddling and looked at me.

"I guess so. We didn't really get to talk, but my dad promised I would be safe. Aunt Tiffany told me that she worked in New York until a few years ago. Her company transferred her to San Francisco. She never got married and said she would love the company." Tara shrugged and set the CD player on her nightstand.

"So, it looks like I'm leaving soon."

"Are you okay with that?" I asked.

She smiled. "I think so. My aunt, um, well, she wants me." Tara popped one of her earpieces in and offered me the other.

I pushed it into my ear. "The Beatles, again?"

"Yes! The Beatles are the best!" Tara exclaimed, pulling the string to shut off the light above her bed.

Bet it's the only CD she has.

At the Monday morning meeting, Melanie told us about her weekend and asked us how the extra outside time was. "Maybe we can do that every Saturday. By the way, we're getting a new kid this afternoon," she said. We watched her leave the room.

Jessica, Tara and Shannon headed to their rooms. Jeff turned on the TV and found Gilligan's Island.

"Jeff," Tommy grumbled, "there has to be something better on than that."

I stood up to go to my room, but Eddy wrapped his arms around my waist and pulled me in tight for a kiss.

I said, "Eddy, you're going to get us in trouble. Hey, what did you tell your mom about us?"

"Nothin' much. Just that I'm worried about what's going to happen to you. Well, that, and I kinda love ya."

Love me?

"What?"

"It's better to give my mom a little info and then let her adjust to it. She'll be fine."

"Yeah, right. Tara's leaving soon."

"Hmm, that's good." He kissed the top of my head and said, "I better get to class. Have fun in art."

When I walked into the art room, Tara, Tommy and Jeff were waiting for me, ready to start working on a wood project.

I sat next to Tara. "Did you get lost?" she teased.

"No, trapped," I laughed.

We pulled the plastic wrap off the wood kit and spread the pieces out.

"Sorry. No hammer or nails, we have to use glue," Stan, the art teacher, announced.

Art was an hour long, and we had the little pre-cut stool built in half that time. Stan let us look through a box of paints. Before the end of class, we placed our stools outside to dry. Mine was mint green with purple hearts stenciled on it, Tara's was purple with green peace signs.

When I went to see Dr. Sue, she was surprised that I was willing to talk about my little sisters without too much prodding. I explained again what they meant to me. I told her about how I fed them and dressed them and read to them. Even though they had their own beds, they slept with me. As I talked, the scratching of her pen started to get on my nerves.

"We only have fifteen minutes left, Sam, and I need to discuss something with you, regarding two notes the staff has in your file."

Uh-oh.

"One, they're worried that you and Eddy are getting too close."

I cracked my knuckles and assured her that we were just good friends. "He's a good listener, Dr. Sue. You did tell me to talk to someone."

We stared at each other for a minute. I was sure she knew Eddy and I had become more than good friends, but I knew if I said anything more, they would separate us.

"I'll accept that for now. But when I suggested you talk to someone about your issues, I meant *me*. And two, they seem to think you plan to run away from here. Please understand, Sam, that there are alarms on every door and cameras in all halls. Eddie has a good life and Tara needs to go with her aunt, so please ... don't ... just don't."

We looked at each other for a minute. I nodded yes and she smiled before saying, "Thank you. You can go."

At dinner, I told Eddy what Dr. Sue had said. Apparently, Eddy was questioned, too, and Tara's and Matt's therapists asked them what was going on.

The new guy walked in and looked for his tray. His pants were held up under his butt with a long belt, and he swam in his oversized T-shirt. He plopped the tray down at the end of our table and sat.

"Hey, I'm Andy."

"Alright, make sure you're up in the morning when Melanie pops her head in. I'm leaving the bathroom light on and shutting the door so she'll think I'm in there. On your way to the dining room, knock twice on his door. If it's safe—," I started.

"I know. I got this," Tara said, and rolled over.

I looked out the crack in the door. At 5:15, Tia, the night guard, grabbed her purse and went to the lobby.

I ducked into the hallway, stopped at the end to peek around the corner, then bolted for Eddy's room.

It was pitch dark and I had to let my eyes adjust for a minute. Matt and Eddy were asleep. I softly touched Eddy's shoulder. He smiled, then opened his covers. I climbed in, snuggling my back against him. He pulled me close.

"Hmm. What time is it?"

"About 5:20. Tara and I have been taking turns watching the night crew. One goes on break at 5:15, but not for long."

"5:20 ... jeez. Go to sleep, Sam," he sighed.

I curled closer and closed my eyes. "Well done, by the way," he added sleepily.

I was tired, but I couldn't sleep. I could feel the hair on my arms raise. No matter what my feelings for Eddy were, it was hard for me to lie this close to someone. I had to move.

I tried to figure out how to wiggle out from under his arm without waking him up. He tightened his grip and murmured, "Hold still, you're fine."

Tara came through as promised, but she didn't knock. She opened the door and said, "Boys, Tommy is going to eat your breakfast if you don't hurry up."

Eddy and I jumped up. Matt rolled over and snored.

"Wow, he sleeps hard," I observed.

"Yeah, he does. See you in a few."

I took a step toward the door, but he grabbed my hand. "Sam, I love you."

I paused. He pulled me close and kissed me softly.

I squeezed him and said, "Love you, too!" Then I slipped out.

Love? Was this love? Or safety? Maybe both ... I have never felt comfortable lying next to someone the way I can with Eddie. Is this love?

At breakfast, our table was really crowded, so we moved all the tables together to form one big one. Melanie came in to give us our 15-minute alert for the morning meeting. As she looked around the room, she broke into a big smile.

It was group therapy day, and no one was thrilled about getting started, so we took our time finishing breakfast.

Since it was Andy's first meeting, we went around the room with introductions. Dr. Sue and Dr. Neal joined us a few minutes later. For some reason, Jeff was on the hot seat. When Dr. Sue asked him to talk about why he was there, he didn't hesitate.

He seemed he loved to surf so much that he'd sleep on the beach for a week or so without telling his parents what he was up to or where he was.

"My parents had police and friends looking for me. When the police found me, they took me to a hospital and called my therapist. I hadn't eaten since I'd left home."

He fidgeted as he went on. "My therapist and my parents think I have a problem, like manic depression or something."

Jeff talked for a few more minutes. When he was quiet, Dr. Sue thanked him and turned to Andy.

The room went silent. Andy fiddled with his ball cap until Dr. Neal said, "Andy, please take the hat off and tell the group why you're here."

Andy slowly pulled the hat off his head. His hair was red, but his eyebrows and lashes were white. He set the cap on his knee and rubbed his hands up and down his pants. His eyebrows bunched together.

Oh, man, I know that feeling.

I swallowed hard and took a deep breath. Eddy and Tara already knew some of my story. I figured I could rescue Andy.

"I'll talk," I offered.

Tara patted my knee.

"Go ahead. What do you wanna know?" I asked.

Dr. Sue tilted her head and pursed her lips. "Well, your story is different, Sam. Maybe you could tell the group what it was like living with your mom. Why don't you start with when she remarried."

I nodded. My hands were shaking. She had so many questions in private therapy, but now *this* is all she wanted me to talk about.

"Well, okay. My mom remarried a few years ago," I began, staring out the window. "He had a good job and plenty of money. Things were okay, as long as the house was clean and quiet. Dishes done. Laundry folded. When he was home, we stayed in our rooms. As long as we didn't bother them, we didn't get hurt."

"Hurt?" Tommy asked.

I ignored him and continued. "Until my mom got pregnant. Then we became dirt. She slept all day while he was at work. Logan and I had to have dinner ready when he got home and my mom seemed to get more and more annoyed by us. His baby was all that mattered.

"After Jackie was born, my mom got really sick and couldn't get out of bed. Logan and I took care of Jackie during the day. My mom wouldn't even feed her. One night after Logan's dad fell asleep, I snuck into his bathroom and took a few bucks. After he went to work the next day, I took Jackie with me to buy formula. Man, was he ticked when he got home that night! I didn't think he would notice a few bucks missing. He did." I took a deep breath and exhaled quickly, remembering the black eye.

"Anyway. Then my mom got pregnant again. Another little girl, Mary. Babies are just too much for her. She just doesn't wanna hold them. I don't even know why she had them. After a while her husband realized there was a problem. He took my mom to a few doctors. I made sure she took the meds he brought home, but it didn't help. I think they even made her worse. She would sleep all day, then get us up at night to redo all the dishes if she found a dirty one in the cupboard or to scrub the floors. The work wasn't so bad. What was hard was trying not to make noise so she wouldn't hit or kick us again."

"When Logan was fifteen, he got a part-time job at Del Taco. After he worked a few months they asked him for his work permit, but he didn't have one. That started some trouble, and Darlene showed up again, and well, here I am."

I studied my hands, regretting that I'd let myself blurt all that out.

"Sam? If your mom was here, what would you ask her?" Dr. Sue asked.

I shook my head. "Nothing."

"So, what trouble did you get into to be put in here?" Jessica asked.

I looked at her and faked a smile. "I was born."

"Sam is not here for being in trouble," Dr. Sue answered. Neither a judge nor a therapist put Sam here."

I could feel everyone's eyes on me, and I wanted to crawl under the couch.

Matt flipped his hair out of his eyes and said, "No wonder you don't talk about your parents. What happened to your dad?"

I was not going there, so I shrugged my shoulders. Tara bumped me with her shoulder, and Eddy nudged me.

"Okay. Someone else talk. I'm done," I stated firmly.

Jessica took over and told us that her parents thought she was out of control. She'd been caught drinking and staying out all night a few times.

"They took me to a counselor, and I told her I was just having fun. But when my mom saw my grades for the last semester, she told the counselor something had to be done. Next thing I knew, my mom pulled in here. My counselor was standing in the doorway with Melanie."

Tara huffed a few times, and I bit back a smile. Eddy took one of his hands out of his pocket and slid it between us. I eased mine next to his, and we linked our pinky fingers. My shaking finally stopped.

When we were dismissed, Dr. Sue caught my attention.

"Sam? Hold on."

"Yeah?" I stopped.

Eddy whispered, "See you after class."

I stood still while Dr. Sue gathered her things, afraid she would ask me to tell her more. Once the room was clear, she said, "Thanks for sharing. I know it was hard for you."

"Sure. But don't expect it again."

Chapter 8

Melanie walked into the dining room, pulled a chair up to the block of tables we had shoved together and set down her clipboard.

"We're going to have our morning meeting while you eat," she said.

That's odd; she normally checks rooms and charts during breakfast.

"I have good news," she continued.

"The center is closing, and we all get a pardon," Andy joked.

"Haha. No. The director has been working on getting a half-day trip approved for you guys. I received an email from him this morning saying that we can take you out today."

"Really?" I asked.

"Yes, really. Now, we have two choices. One: the movies. I printed out what's playing." She shoved a paper toward us, and Jessica started to read it. "Or, two: the beach. They want us back by 12:00. Let's vote so I can make arrangements."

"The beach!" Jeff spouted.

"Surprise there, Jeff," Eddy laughed.

"The beach is an hour drive each way, but I'm game. Well? What do the rest of you think?"

Everyone agreed on the beach. Melanie told us to be ready in ten minutes—beach time was being wasted.

The dining room cleared out, but I stayed put.

This could be my chance to run away. Oh man, I should take my picture and Logan's sweatshirt.

I didn't realize how long I'd been sitting there until Eddy came in looking for me.

"Ready?" he asked.

I huffed, "No."

He pulled up a chair and put an arm around my shoulders.

"This is going to be fun. What's with that face?" he asked.

"What do I wear? I mean, all my clothes look like this, and—"

"Hey, you won't see any of the people at the beach again. Now, let's move out, and don't even think about memorizing street signs."

I scowled, scrunching my face into a tight little knot.

The staff counted us as we piled into the van. Melanie snapped those gray ID bands onto our wrists as the driver turned onto Hwy. 101. The stereo popped on. He searched for a station, stopping when a few of us started to sing along to "This Is How We Do It."

Once the beach was in sight, Melanie reviewed the rules. Each group was assigned a chaperone before we were let out of the van. Eddy grabbed my hand, and we headed for the water with Jeff and Tara. Melanie was walking a few feet behind us.

"I'm gonna sit right here and let the four of you walk. But make sure I can see you. If you can't see me, then I can't see you, and there will be a problem," Melanie scolded. She sat down in the sand and stared after us.

"How'd we get Melanie for our chaperone?" Tara asked.

"Who cares?" Jeff said.

The air was salty, and seagulls were squawking. A few toddlers were building a sandcastle. Their giggling made me think of Jackie and Mary and my heart stung for a minute. We took off our shoes and socks and rolled up our pant legs. I glanced toward the van. Jessica and Shannon were lying on a blanket with their sleeves and pants rolled up. Tommy was throwing a football at Andy, missing, and hitting Matt, who was sitting on a bench. Even I knew there was no way that was an accident! Matt jumped up to chase Tommy.

We walked up and down the little stretch of beach, letting the water run over our feet. I stood still and let it flow around my ankles. The movement made an indentation in the wet sand. When the wave moved out, it felt like the water was dragging you with it; but with my toes dug in, I realized that I hadn't moved. Tara and Jeff went in the water up to their knees. When Eddy started to follow them, I let go of his hand and said I would wait here.

With a playful laugh, he knelt down and motioned for me to do the same. "Let me show you something."

Eddy shoved his hands in the sand. The water washed up over them and then the tide pulled the water out again.

"See those bubbles?"

As the last of the waves rolled beyond us, little shimmers appeared on the surface of the wet sand. Eddy lifted his hands.

"Sand crabs!" he said. He had little sand-colored bug-like things in one hand. I leaned in to see them and shoved my hands in my pockets. In a low, gentle voice, he continued, "They don't bite. See those little bubbles pop up in the sand when the water moves out? Those are the crabs digging in to keep from being washed out to sea."

I'll never walk barefoot on the beach again! Ewww!

He dropped them and they disappeared. A few small brown birds with long legs pecked at the waterline.

Ha! They were after the sand crabs.

No one seemed to care or even notice our group of fully clothed teenagers or the lady in nurse scrubs with a clipboard and cell phone who was watching our every move.

After two glorious hours of pretend freedom, we were loaded into the van and heading back up the 101. We rode in silence except for Jeff. He stared out the window, whispering, "One more week."

"Saturday already," Tara said.

"Yep," Andy answered, like he had been here for months.

"Wonder if she'll visit today," Tara whispered to me.

"Who? Your aunt?"

"She said she would."

Andy and Jessica's therapist came in to see them. They were each gone for half an hour and both came back in a better mood.

Eddy and I played pool against Tara and Jeff. We were kicking their butts, no thanks to me. I was doing a victory dance when Tara stiffened and said, "Look. She's here." Tara's aunt was getting her items checked with the other parents. There was no family therapy during Saturday visitation. No stories. No "How does that make you feel?" Just parents visiting their kids.

Today, I was the only one without a visitor. A hard pit in my stomach turned as families, smiling and laughing, headed for the patio. I was not sure what to do with myself. I couldn't play Skip-Bo alone. Hmm, I could practice pool without anyone watching me. Nah. I headed for my room.

A hand touched my shoulder, and I jumped. "Jeez, don't do that," I said, backhanding Eddy's shoulder.

"Sorry. Wanna sit with us?"

"No thanks, I'm going to call my brother and get some laundry ready," I answered.

"Well, that'll take like 17 minutes. When you're done, come sit with us."

"Okay," I said, but thought *no way*.

I called Logan. "I went to see the girls. They have a live-in caregiver that makes sure Stacy gets her meds. Our sisters are okay."

I fought back tears. Not sure why ... that was *good* news. When he hung up, I held the receiver for a minute before hanging up and heading to my room.

I plopped down on my bed and reached over for the book I'd checked out from the one-shelf library in the schoolroom. I flipped it open to the dog-eared page and glanced at the clock.

Seventeen minutes? Smart-ass. It was more like five.

I watched the time on my clock tick away. It was only noon. Parents would be here for two-to-three more hours. I wondered if Eddy was glad his parents were here. Was he thinking about me? Maybe I should go say hi to Tara's aunt Tiffany.

The lunch cart clanked down the hall. I leaned my head back on my pillow and closed my eyes. I wasn't hungry. At a knock on my door, my eyes popped open. If I didn't answer, maybe whoever it was would go away. The door creaked open a crack and I froze.

"Sam?"

Eddy's mom? Shit!

I got up and opened the door. Eddy was standing there with his mom and dad.

"Hey. Aren't you guys going to eat?" I asked.

"We did; we brought Eddy lunch today," his mom said cheerfully.

"Oh-h."

"I saved you some. Come eat with us," Eddy offered.

"Okay. Um, what is it?"

"Chinese food. It's something different from what you guys eat in here," his mother answered.

"Hmm," I frowned.

"Don't you like Chinese food?" his dad asked.

I shrugged. "Never had it."

They looked at each other like I had said something wrong.

"What? Well, it's still warm. You'll like it," Eddy said.

He picked up my hand and tugged.

When I went to sit down, Eddy pulled my chair out. I stopped and looked at him. "Sorry, is this your seat?" I asked.

He laughed and said, "No, it's yours." Then his dad pulled out his mom's chair and she sat.

Oh. I feel dumb. He's trying to be nice.

Eddy pushed a square white box with red writing toward me. "It's good, Sam—try it."

I popped open the top and frowned. "Are you sure this is good? It smells ... odd."

"It's good. We picked it up on the way here," his dad almost laughed.

I took a deep breath, picked up the plastic fork and took a teensy-tiny bite. It *was* good. I ate a few bites, then stopped. Eddy and his parents were talking like I wasn't there. I felt rude eating in front of them.

When I set down the fork and shut the lid, Eddy said, "Finish it. If you don't, they'll just toss it."

I shook my head and lied. "I'm full."

"Listen, Sam," his mom started, "we can tell that you're more than a friend to Edward."

I froze and looked at Eddy, who was looking at his mother with "please-don't" eyes.

"Oh, please son. We've seen the way you two look at each other. Don't forget, we were young and in love once too," his dad grinned.

"You seem like a nice girl, Sam," his mom continued, "but we were wondering about a few things."

I swallowed hard. "Okay. What?"

"What trouble did you get in?"

I studied the red Chinese writing. *Did it say, "Don't eat this – there will be a catch!"*

"None. My mom left me here."

Eddy put his hand on mine. My face felt flaming hot. *Did they poison me?*

"Hmm, and you're heading for a detention center when your treatment here is complete?" his dad asked.

"Yes. My caseworker is trying to find me a place."

Eddy grumbled something. Our table was silent for a minute.

What were they thinking of me?

I ached to get up and leave.

"Sam, do you believe in God?" Eddy asked suddenly.

I just looked at him.

What? Why would he ask me that in front of them?

My eyes stung and I blinked quickly to stop them from watering. Eddy squeezed my hand.

His mother pushed it. "Well, Sam, do you?"

I didn't look away from Eddy.

How could he put me on the spot like that?

"I don't know much about Him. I'm not sure He's someone I would want to know." I stood up.

Eddy jumped up still holding my hand. "Sam?" I tried to jerk my hand free, but he held on. The stinging in my eyes turned to an intense burning.

"Is that your goal, to lead me to your God and then go back to your safe happy life? God doesn't want me anymore than my mom does!"

I jerked free and stormed away.

"Sam? You okay?" Tara asked, walking into our room.

I shook my head.

"My aunt just left. Do you want to play Skip-Bo?" she asked, cards in hand.

"Did all the parents leave?" I asked, looking out from under my pillow.

"No. They have another hour. Have you been alone this whole time?"

"No. I was with Eddy and his family for a while." I sat up and pulled my hair into a scrunchy.

Tara plopped next to me. "What happened?"

"Eddy asked if I believe in God. In front of his parents! I was so mad that I can't even remember what I said. They must think I'm the devil."

She put her hand on my shoulder, and I tensed, so she removed it.

"Oh, I doubt they think that. You're far from the Devil! God is great. I believe in Him. You don't?"

Stacy saw nothing but evil in me, why would anyone see something else.

I rolled my eyes. "No, I don't. Now deal, and no cheating this time," I demanded, pulling myself together.

"Cheat? Me?" she asked in mock innocence and put a card on the bed in front of me.

We ate in silence. When I started to rip my dinner roll into small pieces, Eddy asked, "Can I talk to you? Alone?" He got up, grabbed our trays and stuck them in the cart.

I hesitated.

Oh, shit! He's mad. Why? Because I told him I didn't want anything to do with his stupid God!? I followed him to the TV area but turned and went over to the dryer.

I opened the door, pulled out my shirt, and started to fold it. He reached from behind me and took it. I turned and faced him. "You're mad?"

"Yeah," he said.

I tensed up, waiting for him to hit me. He was a big guy, and I was sure it would hurt. Instantly, I was embarrassed to think that about him.

"Because I don't want to know your God?"

"No, I'm mad because, well, how could you think for one minute that I was trying to trick you into believing in God? Haven't you heard a word I've said to you?" He spoke calmly, but I could hear the anger in his voice.

I stiffened and took a step back. My throat burned and I felt it start to knot.

No, you don't.

I inhaled slowly and the urge to cry eased up.

"You never asked me about God before, and I thought it was some sorta intervention. Kinda hurt coming from you." My words came out throaty and muffled.

He took a step toward me. I took a step back.

"Jeez, Sam, I'm not going to hurt you. And I wasn't tricking you. My mom wanted to know; I thought it was better if I was the one to ask you. I understand where you are right now. I do love you, Sam, and hurting you was not my intention." He took another step toward me, and this time I stayed put. Eddy pulled me into a hug, and instantly the tightness left my body.

"I'm sorry," I mumbled into his chest.

"Well. I didn't think *anything* rattled you. Kinda nice to see some emotion," he teased.

He kissed the top of my head, and I giggled in relief. "I think your mom put something in that stinky food."

"Chinese food," he said, letting me go and pulling me to the couch. We found *The Simpsons.*

I sat curled up next to him for a minute, then asked, "What does your dad do? You said your mom stays home with you and your brother."

"He's a cardiologist," he responded.

"Oh, a cardiologist?"

He smiled. "A heart doctor."

"And your brother, what's he like?"

Eddy paused, like he was looking for the right word. "He's a punk. Kind of a jerk, too. I guess I should give him more credit, it's just that he's always following me around asking questions. Like someone I know. Anything else, Nosey?"

"Yes."

He raised his eyebrows.

"What do you want to be when you grow up?" I asked, I never thought about what I wanted to be, but for some reason, I figured he had.

He smiled. "A pediatric neurosurgeon. The brain fascinates me and I like kids. They keep it real. You?"

"I'm not sure. Hey. You have to be good at school for something like that. Right?"

"Yeessss," he answered.

Jeff and Tara walked in "Cool. *The Simpsons*," Jeff exclaimed. Tommy yelled from the living room, "Who's playing?"

Eddy gave me a crooked smile and got up. Shannon started to flip channels.

"I hate *The Simpsons*," she grumbled.

I jumped up and went back to the dryer, folded the shirt on top, and pulled out another.

How different can Eddy and I be?

Chapter 9

"Samantha."

"It's Sam," I muttered.

Dr. Sue was standing in the dining room doorway. I stiffened and dropped my spork on my breakfast tray. *Oh, no! My sisters?*

I tried to talk without sounding shaky. "Wow, Dr. Sue, you're never here this early."

"Sam, we need to talk."

"I know, it's Monday."

"I have a busy day and decided to get here early to talk to you."

My mind raced as I followed her down the hall. What could be so important that she had to come early? Could my mom have done something to my girls? Was this about Eddy and me?

When we got to the office she directed me in first and closed the door. Then she flipped open my file and put her little square glasses on.

"You seem to be doing better," she said.

"Yes, I think so."

"I have some sad news." She said, taking off her glasses. I fidgeted in my seat. "I know that you and Tara have become very good friends."

"Yes. Did we do something wrong?"

"You tell me, did you?" I froze. Silence.

"No, I can't think of anything," I said, staring out the window.

"Good. I wanted to tell you that Tara's aunt is on her way to pick her up."

I bit my lower lip and whispered, "She's leaving? Today?"

"Yes, in a few hours. Melanie called me yesterday around noon. I planned to come last night after my private practice appointments to let you know. Melanie suggested I wait until today." She put her glasses back on and looked at me from above them. "Any idea why the staff didn't want to tell you and Tara? Yesterday?"

"No. Ma'am," I said.

Oh, crap! They know we've talked about running away. But I think we're past that decision.

She raised one eyebrow and smiled a tight, knowing smile. "Well, let's get some work done so you can help her pack."

My sisters' Mary and Jackie's dad seemed to be the topic for today. Did he hit me? Did he touch me in ways he shouldn't have? Lastly, where did he go? I wouldn't answer the last two. I watched the clock, and as it got close to an hour, I asked, "Did Darlene find a place for me yet?"

"There' s a detention center ready for you. But I called a place out of state that would be a better option. We are still working on it."

"Is it a detention center too?" I asked, tensely. My peaceful lake and cabin stared at me. I counted the trees that framed the lake.

"No, Sam. We're trying to find a safer, more appropriate place for you. Hour's up. You may go to your room, then class."

I stood up and headed for the door. When I looked back, she had closed my file and was squeezing her temples. I left her door open.

When I walked into our room, Tara was sitting on her bed.

"Did Dr. Sue tell you?"

"Yeah. You okay?" I sat on my bed facing her.

"I think so. Dr. Neal came to get me after you left. I've been here two long months and didn't think this would be how I would feel about leaving."

"What? Happy?"

"No, it's odd. Happy and nervous and sad at the same time. This place is … safe. I've got a groove here, ya know? But my dad signed me over to my aunt. It's all legal."

"Well, you said your aunt wants you. That's kinda cool. Maybe we can write to each other."

"Maybe. Hey, when Eddy saw Dr. Neal come to get me, he asked what we did to attract attention. I told him we had done nothing, but as I left the room, I heard Matt creating some great story. Melanie said that after her announcement about me leaving, the morning meeting was very quiet." Tara laughed.

"Matt has a great imagination when it comes to trouble. So does Tommy."

"Yep, gonna miss that. Hey. The night staff overheard us talking. Dr Neal said they knew we planned to run. They plan to keep an eye on doors. Just the exterior door as best I can tell," she warned me.

"Okay, thanks. Do you need help packing?"

"No, I'm packed. You'd better get to class."

"Tara, your aunt is ready," Darlene announced, standing in the doorway.

Tara had filled a suitcase and had to put a few things in her backpack. She squared her shoulders and led the way out of our room. Everyone gathered to say goodbye and exchange phone numbers.

Tara pressed a piece of paper into my hand with her aunt's address and phone number. Then she put her cases down and hugged me tightly for a long minute. I stood stiff as a statue, not sure how to respond. Eddy was standing behind her watching me. He winked at me and moved his arms like he was hugging the air. I reached up with one hand and patted Tara's back. He gave me an "Oh, jeez!" smirk and rolled his eyes.

Tara turned and gave Eddy a shoulder punch. "Take care of her," she ordered.

"Of course!" he said, lifting her off the ground in a big bear hug. Tara giggled.

"I can take care of myself," I grumbled.

"I know." She handed me the handmade necklace that I had seen on her dresser the day I arrived.

"What? No, Tara, I can't take this," I said, pushing her hand away.

"You can and will ... I made it when I got here. I want you to have it."

With that, the first friend I'd ever had walked out the door.

My room was too quiet that night. No music, no light snoring. Her bed was already stripped and remade. Her dresser, cleaned. Nothing but a pair of PJ pants and my necklace left to show she was ever here. I felt a hard lump form in my throat; I missed her already.

I pulled the string above my bed and the room went dark.

At midnight, my door opened and closed.

"Scoot over."

"I told you they're watching me," I hissed.

"Pssh. They don't think you'll try to run away alone. I heard them talking," Eddy whispered. He curled up behind me.

Alone.

I wiped a tear off my cheek and fell into asleep before I could say a word.

Melanie caught my arm, as I walked out of art. She handed me a thick envelope that had been opened and was barely taped shut.

"You got a letter."

I went to my room and sat on my bed. When I turned it over to see who sent it, an Abba-Zaba fell onto my blanket. A huge smile took over my face. I smelled the yellow-taxi-cab wrapper. *Ahhh.* I loved Abba-Zabas, the soft vanilla taffy wrapped around creamy peanut butter. But the only way to eat them without losing teeth was to freeze them and break them into pieces.

I pulled out the note.

> Sam,
> Hope you are doing ok. Thought you would like an Abba-Zaba.
> I am doing fine. Stay strong.
>
> > Your brother,
> > Logan

I looked at the letter for a minute, then set it in my drawer and grabbed my Abba-Zaba.

As I passed the staff station, I asked, "Melanie, can I put this in the freezer."

"Better put your name on it. And hurry up; you're late for class," she said.

Jessica and Shannon were talking about some movie they'd seen. "Oh, my God! He is hot." I heard Shannon gush.

Eddy came in and grabbed his stuff. When he sat next to me, I asked him why he wasn't with his group.

"I don't know. I just left Dr. Neal and Melanie told me to come to this class." He shrugged and started his work.

I glanced at his book. "What's that?" I whispered.

"Calculus," he whispered back, not taking his eyes away from the book. He reached under the table and squeezed my hand.

Calculus. He was waiting for college acceptance letters and I had not gone to school since the third grade. We were so different.

He finished that page and then worked on two more. Looking over at my worksheet, which was only half done, he asked, "You okay?"

I scowled. "I'm not stupid."

He set his hand over my paper. "Didn't say you were. But you look at that sheet for a minute, read some of that book, then look at that sheet again. If you're having trouble, I can help."

Jeez, I felt dumb enough without sitting next to Mr. Smarty-Pants. I blew out a deep breath and nodded. Much as I didn't want his stinkin' help, I needed it. He showed me how to do the math problems as if he were my parent or teacher.

When the sheet was done, I teased, "Thanks, Dad."

"Darlene checked on your sisters. She said the new caregiver is great and your ... Stacy is taking her meds every day. Darlene and the caregiver made a list of family members that we can call to see if you can stay with them."

"Family?"

Dr. Sue bit her pen and said "Yes, family. Your grandma said she can't take you right now."

"My grandma?" I asked, feeling my forehead crease in confusion.

"Yes. I talked to her, your mom's sisters and your great Aunt. She's your mom's aunt, your grandma's sister. She wants to think it over and will call me back."

Stacy has sisters?

"She might be great. You won't know if we don't try."

"She's related to my mom. How great can she be?" I sighed.

Dr. Sue looked at me for a minute before answering. "She was very nice, Sam. It's good to be aware of all of your options."

I nodded.

After dinner, I sat cross-legged on the washing machine, with my right elbow on my knee and my face cradled in my hand.

The guys were playing cards and the girls were painting their nails. Eddy came around the corner of the laundry area and said, "There you are. How you doin'?"

"Just waiting for the buzzer." He stood close enough that if it had been anyone else, I would have scooted back.

"Do you miss Tara?"

"Yeah."

"You're very quiet. Missing your sisters? Logan?"

"Yeah. I do. The idea of not seeing them anytime soon sucks," I mumbled, which was not what I was thinking about, at least not at that moment. I was trying to remember Aunt Donna.

Eddy leaned against the washer and pulled me closer. "It does suck, but you'll see them when you can."

I wanted to tell him that there was no way he could understand what I was going through, but instead I hugged him and gave him a quick kiss on the neck, then jumped off the washer.

Chapter 10

"Happy Birthday, Ms. Rain," Eddy said, when I sat next to him.

I scrunched my eyes shut and squeezed my lips together. "Oh, man. How did you know?"

I had heard kids at school talking about their birthday parties, filled with cake and balloons. I never went to one and I certainly never deserved a party. No party. No presents. And no cake.

Who told him anyway?

Eddy raised his eyebrows, like he heard what I was thinking.

"Melanie. She asked if you said anything about it being your 16th birthday."

"No! They aren't going to sing are they?

Eddy tilted his head and frowned. "Not if you don't want them to. But we do have something planned."

My eyes shot open. "We? Does everyone know?"

He nodded, then took my toast. I pushed my tray in front of him and sat back, crossing my arms. He shook his head and teased, "Are you pouting?"

"I didn't want anyone to know. Why did she have to open her big mouth?"

"She was worried you would be upset if no one said anything."

Crap. It would have to be on a Saturday when parents are visiting. Great!

"Did you tell your pare—"

"Yep," He smirked.

I got up and left without putting my tray on the cart. I flipped on the TV and found something to watch. The blood raced through my heart like a freight train. I didn't want any birthday attention. He came over and sat next to me, leaning forward to kiss me. I put my hand up to stop him.

"I don't want anyone to know about my birthday."

"Too late; they know."

"But it's not a big deal and—"

"Sam, they know. Mike even got permission for us to bake a cake."

I just stared at him.

"Come on, we all want cake, and your birthday is something I want to celebrate." He gave my knee a squeeze and paused. "Let it go and enjoy the day."

I gave him a quick peck. "Eddy, it is just another day."

"Not anymore." he answered cheerfully, drinking some juice.

Tommy and Matt came in arguing about the name of the Oakland Raiders' quarterback. They stopped abruptly when they saw me and started belting out: "Happy birthday to you, you live in a zoo . . ."

My face turned red, and I mouthed *thanks* to Eddy. Fighting back a smile, he winked. After the morning meeting and another sappy round of "Happy Birthday to You," Jennifer escorted us to the kitchen. It was huge, full of metal shelves and oversized refrigerators, stoves and ovens. Some staff were still cleaning up the breakfast trays.

A gray-haired lady stopped wiping off the steel counter and asked, "So, who is the birthday girl?"

I shrugged when everyone pointed to me.

"Well, happy birthday. Chocolate or vanilla?" she asked.

"Chocolate."

She slid a huge silver bowl toward us. "Wash your hands and put on aprons." She pointed to a row of aprons hanging on the wall. We each grabbed one and Jennifer handed us hairnets.

"Yeah, right," Tommy said, handing the hairnet back. The other workers snickered, but didn't stop working.

"Eggs?" Eddy said, jabbing me with his elbow.

Trying to be a good sport, I put my big-girl smile on and cracked the eggs over the bowl. We all added something and took turns using the mixer.

Mike walked in and asked, "Am I too late?"

"Nope," Jennifer answered.

He handed Eddy a little bag and said, "Good. I was hoping to make it in time. Happy birthday, Sam!"

Eddy handed me the bag and said, "Happy birthday, Samantha Rain."

I looked at him and bit my lower lip.

"Open it," Jeff commanded.

I pulled the ribbon off the bag handle and looked inside first and then at Eddy as I pulled out a disposable camera.

"You got me a camera?" I said, a smile creeping onto my face.

"Not much of a present, but we wanted to get you something," Eddy said, waving his hand toward the rest of the kids.

"It's a great present. No one has ever gotten me a present before," I told them.

Eddy's face fell.

Shit. I shouldn't have said that.

Jennifer broke the silence by taking the camera from me and clicking some photos of all of us baking the cake. We poured the batter into a big square pan.

"I'll take it out and let it cool. It'll be iced by dinner," the kitchen lady told us as we hung up our aprons.

Mike shoved his hand out for my birthday present. I hesitated, then handed it to him.

"I'll return it when you're released," he said.

"You guys have 45 minutes. Behave. See you all Monday," Mike waved. We followed Jennifer back into the center.

The smell of Jessica painting her nails overwhelmed the TV room. I flipped open one of Jeff's magazines and started reading. Jennifer was braiding Shannon's hair. I missed my Skip-Bo partner. Jessica stood up to leave the room and stopped.

"Jeez! Were you hungry? There's nothing left of your nails!" she said, grabbing my hand. I yanked it back.

"What's wrong with them?"

"Okay. Get comfortable. This is going to take me some time," Jessica stated. She sat next to me and grabbed my hand. When I tried to pull it away, she tightened her grip and smiled. "It won't hurt. Just watch TV."

I fidgeted while she filed and buffed my nails then slathered my hands with lotion. It seemed like an hour before she set my hands down.

"Thanks," I said and started to get up.

"Hey, I'm not done. Pick a color, I only have three. Hurry. Parents get here soon."

I rolled my eyes and pointed to one of the little bottles in her hand.

"Of course. I should have known." Jessica frowned and set down the bright-pink nail polish.

I was waving limp hands with fresh nail polish back and forth as the parents were walking in.

Jessica handed her stuff to Jennifer and bounced over to hug her mom. They walked out to the patio, arms linked. Her mom was smiling from ear to ear.

Does my mom miss me at all?

I went into the dining area and pulled my Abba-Zaba out of the freezer, snapping it into pieces before opening the wrapper.

"What is that?" Eddy's dad asked.

"Hello, Dr. Pattin. It's an Abba-Zaba. Wanna try it?"

He sat next to me, and I moved the open wrapper toward him. "Well, you tried our Chinese food so ... okay, I'll try your Abba-Zaba." He popped a small piece into his mouth.

"Where are Eddy and his mom?" I asked, while he chewed.

"His mom's talking to Matt's dad. I saw you sitting in here. Alone."

We were silent for a minute. He said, "This is very chewy. I'll bet dentists love these things." We both laughed.

"What did we miss?" Eddy's mom asked, as she walked in with Eddy at her side.

"Nothing," we both chimed. Eddy's dad swallowed hard. I wrapped up the rest of my candy bar.

Eddy and I followed his parents out to the patio and over to the same green table we'd sat at last time. His parents asked about our week. Mrs. Pattin set out plates and containers of food they'd brought. Chicken.

Phew! Normal stuff.

"This is good. Does your mom always cook like this?" I asked, looking at Eddy.

"Oh, my, no," she gasped, and looked at me like I had just said the "F" word. "This is from Kentucky Fried Chicken. Eddy likes it."

Eddy and his dad were both enjoying their lunch, but his mom seemed upset. "Samantha?" she asked.

"Yes?"

"Sam, Eddy is going home soon. Did he tell you?"

I looked at Eddy and felt my heart stop and then start again.

"No."

"The judge sent him here for six weeks. They felt that was long enough for him to learn his lesson," his dad added.

Eddy's mom lowered her chin and glared at him with bullet eyes.

"Yes, ma'am. Vacation's over," Eddy acknowledged.

"Of course, he can call you while you're here, but he won't be permitted to visit."

I swallowed hard and looked at Eddy, feeling my face get hot. "I know; he's not family."

"Right. Do you want me to get you a calling card so you can call him?" she asked.

Eddy shook his head. "Mom? I told you, I wanna get her a cell phone. Nothing fancy. A TracFone maybe."

The three of them looked at each other for a minute as if they were having an unspoken conversation.

"She doesn't know where she's going, Dad," he pleaded.

"Well Eddy, you have a job and can pay for it, right?" his dad queried.

"Of course, Dad."

"No. I don't want you to pay for—" I began to say.

Ignoring me, Eddy asked, "Okay, then. Can you bring it next visit?"

His dad nodded and their conversation moved on to Paul, Eddy's little brother. He had joined a band and was practicing a lot, which his mom didn't seem to like.

"Your dad is thinking about letting them practice in the guest house. The noise from the garage is annoying," she explained. Eddy was listening intently.

"You have a guest house?" I asked. They stopped talking and stared at me.

Eddy leaned over and whispered, "It's more like a studio apartment. We use it when we have company." Eddy reached under the table and squeezed my knee. I flinched.

"Coach called to see when you'd be back," his dad mentioned.

"Hockey coach?" I asked and Eddy smiled. "Yes. I can't wait to get back on the ice."

"Sam. You have a phone call at the staff station," Jennifer yelled from the doorway.

I froze. "My mom?" I sprinted to the staff station, and Jennifer handed me the phone through the open plexiglass window.

"Hello," I said, the anxiety rising in my voice like steam in a tea kettle.

"Hey! Happy birthday, little sister! Sorry, I can't come to see you," Logan said cheerfully.

I didn't know how to feel. Part of me was glad Logan remembered, but another part of me had hoped that my mom would.

"That's alright. Eddy and his parents are sitting with me. I'm so glad you called." We talked for five minutes before Logan had to get to the pizza place where he worked.

The cake was on top of the rolling cart when dinner came in. After dinner, the staff let us take our pieces of cake into the TV room and we watched *Beverly Hills Cop*. I took a small bite, then felt my eyebrows raise as I shoved my fork into the cake for another bite, and exclaimed, "Wow this is good!" Eddy laughed.

That night, I laid in my room thinking about Tara, hoping she was doing all right with her aunt. I wanted to tell her about Eddy leaving soon. My eyes stung and my face burned. I rolled over to check the time: 10:30. My mom hadn't called. I knew she wouldn't, but I wanted her to. A warm tear streamed down my cheek. I didn't bother to wipe it away. I tried to think about Eddy's parents. I bet they'd had a great childhood. I bet they were never afraid to shut their eyes.

I closed my eyes tight, to try to get myself under control and stop the gush of tears. That only made it worse.

I could hear my mom screaming about a dirty cup she had found on the coffee table, her bare feet heading toward my room. Without bothering to turn on the light, she grabbed my hair and pulled me out of bed. My hands grasped at her hands as I struggled to get my feet under my body. She pulled me to the kitchen.

"You will never go to bed with this house looking like this again," she shouted.

I didn't dare tell her that I had checked before I went to bed and that cup wasn't there. Nothing was out of place. She let me go and started pulling the dishes out of the cupboards, all the while yelling about how worthless I was. She threw some cups, and a few hit me.

"You will wash every frickin' dish in this house until you get it right, you little bitch!"

Once the cupboards were empty, she left the kitchen. The floor was covered in clean dishes, and I started to gather them up, knowing that was not the end of it.

She always came back, madder than when she had left. Each time she returned with something different—a curtain rod, a vacuum cleaner cord, a belt—to hit me with.

My eyes flew up to darkness. I grabbed at the string above my bed to turn on the light.

It was so cold, I couldn't stop shaking. I wanted to take the blanket off Tara's bed, but I was too cold to move. I tried to think of the warm sun, but it didn't work.

My door creaked open.

Shit! It's her! No!

I squeezed my eyes and tried to quiet my breathing.

Stop! It can't be her. She's not here!

"Sam?" Eddy whispered.

"Eddy." I sighed with relief.

The bed dipped as he pulled up the covers and climbed in behind me. I tensed up when his arm slid over me.

"Jeez, you're shaking. Shhh. What happened?"

He doesn't need to know. He won't understand.

I leaned into him and tried to take a deep breath. It stung my lungs to breathe. He moved the other arm, and I picked up my head so he could fit it in.

"Tighter," I stuttered, my voice sounding like a little kid.

He shifted my body into his and wrapped both arms around me.

"You're safe now. You can sleep, Babe," he whispered as he kissed the back of my head.

I linked my fingers in his and finally my body got warm and heavy.

Chapter 11

Dr. Sue put on her little square glasses and spoke matter-of-factly, almost like she was dictating into a recorder. "I called your Aunt Donna. She's not interested in having you come live with them, but she's willing to help come up with other options for you."

Her voice seemed miles away as I imagined living in that log cabin.

"Sam? Did you hear me?" she asked.

"Yes, ma'am. Do you think my mom remembered my birthday?"

She put her pen down and took her glasses off. I glanced at her and thought she'd look a lot younger if she didn't pull her hair back into such a tight bun.

"I don't know, Sam. I meant to stop in on Saturday. I'm sorry. Happy belated birthday."

"No biggie."

"Donna is going to talk to her husband and call me tonight with any ideas. I told her how far you have come in the six weeks you have lived here and that you were a good kid who just needed somewhere safe to stay."

She pulled a few sheets of paper out of her briefcase and handed them to me. "I need you to complete these. Do your best. I'll be back tomorrow morning for them." With that, Dr. Sue dismissed me.

I rolled the papers into a tube without looking at them. Matt and Tommy were playing pool against Jeff and Andy. I went to the kitchen and pulled my Abba-Zabba from the freezer. I dropped the roll of papers on the dining-room table, running my hands hard against the papers to flatten them. "Application to Boys Town" appeared in bold black letters across the top.

Eddy, Tommy and Jeff walked in, grabbed something to drink and sat at the table. Eddy kissed the top of my head and said, "What's this?" He moved the papers in front of him.

"Dr. Sue asked me to fill them out," I replied, taking a drink.

"Did she call Aunt Donna?" he asked, his eyes not moving off the papers. Tommy and Andy snatched a piece of candy and looked at the application too.

"Donna's going to call Dr. Sue tonight with some ideas. I guess this is another option." I shrugged.

Eddy pressed his thumb to the lines on my forehead. "I can help you with this if you want," he said, turning the page.

Smarty pants!

"Sure. What is Boys Town? I'm not a boy," I stated, taking it from him.

"It's a group home for unwanted teenagers. It says here that it was originally for orphaned boys, but they started accepting girls in 1979. You have to write an essay, too."

His warm breath on my ear made me flinch. "You're not going there. Not even for one night, Babe."

The lunch cart came rumbling in, and the guys jumped up for their tray.

Mrs. Herzog started handing out work. Matt and Shannon were talking about what was the best *Star Wars* movie. Matt's mouth gaped as Shannon dismissed the great battle scenes and went on and on instead about Princess Leia's relationship with Luke. I tried not to laugh every time Matt rolled his eyes. Part of me wanted to ask what the movie was about, but I decided now was not the time.

Eddy pushed his books and papers to the side. He ripped a sheet of paper out of his spiral notebook and moved the application between us. "Here," Eddy said, "write your answers on this scratch paper, then copy them to the application. That's what I do."

Are you going to tell me what happened last night? was written across the top in neat Eddy-style writing.

Just a bad dream, I wrote below it. He shook his head and opened one of his thick books.

I started working on the application. Every once in a while, Eddy would stop his work and look at mine.

"Nebraska?" He sighed, when I got to the last page.

"What? It's in Nebraska?" I whispered.

"That's what it says. Boys Town, Nebraska." He pointed to the bottom of the page and gave me a worried grin.

"Hmmm, it's cold in Nebraska," I observed. He didn't look amused.

"Just go through the motions."

He looked over all my answers, making spelling and grammar corrections. Then I copied it to the application.

For the first time, I was glad to see Dr. Sue, mainly because she pulled me out of music class. Today's lesson was on reading music and they might as well have been trying to teach me to read Chinese.

"Did you complete that packet yesterday?" Dr. Sue asked as she flipped open my file.

"Yes."

"I need to fax it today. The director of admissions in Boys Town is waiting for it. If you qualify, they'll have a bed for you in four weeks."

My heart felt like it was in my throat. "Do I stay here until they're ready for me? If I get in?"

"No." Dr. Sue turned to me, taking off her glasses and setting them on her desk. Then she rolled her seat closer, her knees almost touching mine. I squirmed and tried to put more space between us.

"Sam. I talked to Aunt Donna last night. She lives on a ranch with her husband. Their daughter and her husband live there too. They talked it over and are willing to let you stay with them until your spot is available at Boys Town."

"Really?" I asked, not sure I'd heard her correctly.

A smile formed across her face. "Really. All four of them work and they don't have any kids. This isn't permanent, but they want to help, and I suggest you do whatever they ask of you."

"Are they nice?"

"They seem to be."

"Dr. Sue, is Boys Town in Nebraska?"

"Yes, it is. But it's not a detention center. I think it's better for you than the other options. Donna and her husband will be here to meet you on Thursday. Do you have any questions? Any concerns?"

"No. Well, um, does my mom know that I'm going to Nebraska?"

She took a deep breath and nodded. "Yes. Darlene called her."

"Okay. Are my sisters—?"

"Darlene is all over it."

I nodded and looked at the cabin in the picture. If only I could crawl inside it and disappear.

"I'm sorry, but I have to go. I have appointments at my private practice. Is there anything else you need to talk about?"

"No, I'm good."

"Okay. I should get going."

What did she mean Darlene was all over it? Did she remove my sisters? Shit!

The pool cues clanking against the table snapped me back. I spun around to tell Eddy about my aunt, but I didn't see him. The music/art room door was open, which was odd. I wandered in and there he was, sitting at the piano. His eyes were closed and he was playing something that made my mouth drop. Ms. Sandy was leaning back against the wall watching him.

He stopped playing and opened his eyes, smiling when he saw me.

"One more?" He asked, turning to Ms. Sandy.

"Please. How long have you been playing, Eddy?" she asked, leaning against a table near the piano.

"Forever," he said.

Eddy tapped the bench he was sitting on and motioned to me with his head. I went to sit next to him.

"Have you ever played?" he asked.

I rolled my eyes.

Seriously?

"Sorry," he mumbled. He ran his long fingers across the keys. His voice interrupted the music. "My pap taught me this one."

"Wow. How did you learn?"

"I just told you. My pap. He could play piano in his sleep," he said. A group gathered in the doorway and we listened until he stopped playing.

When he stopped, he bumped me with his shoulder. "Dinnertime."

He thanked Ms. Sandy on our way out of the music room. She told him he could play anytime and asked him if he realized how good he was. He nodded, pushing his lips into a straight line.

Whoa. What was that all about?

"Did Dr. Sue hear from Donna?" he asked when we got to the hallway.

"Yep and she's faxing my application today." His forehead creased when he asked, "Donna didn't have better ideas?"

"Well, kinda."

He stopped walking. "And?"

I tried to sound calm as I filled him in. He didn't take his eyes off me as he listened. When I stopped, he said, "I see. And you would rather not tell me what happened last night?"

"Just a bad dream. I get them," I answered, dropping my eyes to my hands.

He pulled up my chin, forcing me to look at him, "You were a mess. Tell me."

I narrowed my eyes and pushed the words through my teeth.

"I had a bad dream; that's all."

Chapter 12

Dinner was almost over, and parents would arrive soon. I wanted to hide.

"What's up, Sam?" Eddy asked.

"Do you think they'll show up?" I pushed my green beans around my plate, making little piles and then spreading them out. I wondered if I would ever see my sisters again.

"Oooh, are you scared?" Matt mocked.

"No!" I snapped, picking up a green bean and throwing it at him.

"Yes, you are," Tommy said, eyeing my tray.

"You don't need to worry," Jessica said reassuringly.

"Sam. Eat something, please." Eddy begged.

My stomach was doing flips. I ate a green bean then slid my tray toward Tommy.

"Hey, where's Jeff?" I asked, hoping to take the attention off me.

"I haven't seen him since lunch," Tommy offered, taking a bite of my chicken.

"Odd. Huh! Wonder where he is." I followed Eddy to the TV room.

He flipped through channels before plopping next to me. He kissed the back of my hand, then set it down on his leg. The opening credits to *The A-Team* had his full attention.

"What's with you?" I asked.

He shrugged. "Just thinking, I'm leaving in two days and have no clue what's going to happen to you."

"Well, I'll be here for at least another week."

"I go back to school Monday, back to work Wednesday. Back on the ice Saturday. My same friends. Same house. I can't imagine how you feel."

"It's not like I have a choice."

His forehead wrinkled up and he shook his head slowly.

"Hey, Eddy? Do you think you are, I don't know, who you are because of your parents?"

He linked his fingers with mine, but kept an eye on *The A-Team*.

"I never thought about it but, yes. They've given my brother and me so much. They didn't just *say* they loved us, they showed us. My dad took us on adventure walks on the beach, my mom read to us, and they've been at every one of our games." His lips curled up at the corners.

I studied his fingers, the way they wrapped around mine. "So, are you more like your mom or your dad?"

"I'm told my dad, I have the same drive."

"Eddy. I must be like my mom then. I mean, I don't know my dad. So, who do I take after?"

He blinked a few times before his eyes met mine.

"I think you can be whoever you want to be. You have a clean slate. You know what I mean. Like a do-over?"

"Yeah. Clean. But with no chalk to write with."

He laughed. "I think Donna will get you some chalk. If not, I will. A big multi-colored pack." He turned his attention back to the character B.A., who was blowing up things.

I took a deep breath and pretended to watch the TV.

Mr. T was building some movable army fort out of nothing. Eddy explained how and that it would work.

I tried not to laugh when I exclaimed, "Oh, Eddy! That could only work on TV."

Tommy and Andy came in and Tommy said, "Oh, this is a good one. Mr. T hates to fly. They drug him. Watch." Eddy rolled his eyes.

"Hey Sam? What's your favorite food?" Eddy asked when the show was over.

"What?" I asked, my eyebrows practically knitted together at his out-of-the-blue question.

"I wanna know more about you. So?"

"Hmmm. Well, I don't know. What's yours?"

"That's easy. Japanese. Hands down, the best," he said, like he had been asked that before.

"Argh. Gross. You eat raw fish?" My face scrunched up at the thought.

"No." He laughed. "That's sushi. I'm talking about rice. Steak. Chicken. *Cooked* shrimp. They make it all in front of you with fire and tricks. I have to take you. So, what's your favorite thing to eat?"

I looked at him for a minute, scanning my memory.

I don't know. Food was not for fun; it was for survival.

"Well. Before Logan left, he worked at Del Taco. He brought home food sometimes. That was good."

Eddy's eyes got wide as he said, "Reheated Del Taco. Wonderful."

"I didn't say it was reheated," I teased.

His hand cupped my cheek. "We can do better than that. Parents will be here any minute. Are you ready?"

I sucked air through my teeth. "Ready as I'll ever be."

Parents started to file into the center. I took my spot against the wall where I could see the main door. I wanted to see Aunt Donna come in, if she even showed up. No new faces arrived and Jeff was still missing.

Dr. Sue and Dr. Neal started the meeting, and I tried to ignore the fact that my aunt was not here. When I heard Jeff's name, my attention shifted to Dr. Sue as she explained that Jeff was discharged while we were in class. He didn't want to deal with goodbyes. I had to admit that made me kinda sad, but it didn't surprise me. I glanced at the door. Still no Aunt Donna.

Tommy explained that he only did drugs to improve his football stats. His dad sternly told him that he would rather see him clean than see him be the star quarterback on drugs.

The door hadn't moved. No new visitors.

Crap! They don't want me.

Once family therapy was over, I bolted for my room, pulled the picture of my sisters out of my drawer and plopped down on my bed.

There was a knock at my door.

"Sam?"

I set down the photo.

Please leave me alone. I just want some time to regroup.

"Sam, we know you're in here." The door creaked open and Melanie's head popped around the corner.

"Hey, I want to introduce you to a few people. Can we come in?"

"I guess," I said reluctantly.

She swung the door open, Melanie and Dr. Sue walked in, followed by a man and a woman. They looked older than my mom, but not old. Not like they could be my mom's parents or anything.

"Sam, this is your Aunt Donna and her husband, Frank,"

Aunt Donna was pretty, her hair styled to frame her face, her little gold glasses more like face jewelry than glasses. Her clothes were put together well, with everything matching and fitting nicely.

"Hello, Sam," she said.

She walked hesitantly toward me like I was a trapped feral cat.

"Do you remember me? You were at my house once for a Christmas party."

I didn't want to hurt her feelings, so I whispered, "Yes," even though I had no clue who she was.

Her husband said, "Sam, I'm Frank." No doubt stuck for words, he repeated what his wife had said. "You came to my house once for a Christmas party."

My mind was racing faster than a racecar as I tried to trace back my memories. "Please sit down," I urged, feeling very rude for not offering sooner. They sat together on Tara's empty bed and Dr. Sue sat next to me on mine.

I scanned them again, trying to recall some memory of them. Something about their kind faces made me *want* to remember.

Frank was dressed in a button-up shirt tucked into belted tan jeans. He was wearing just the right amount of aftershave, musky but not strong. His gray hair was brushed smoothly and parted on the right.

"Sam. We aren't young anymore," Donna began gently, "but we are willing to let you stay with us for a month. Dr. Sue said you need a safe place to stay while you're waiting for a more permanent place." Her voice was calm and she spoke gently and with love.

Where did my mom get her hatred from? Oh, that's right. Me!

"We share the ranch with our daughter Haley and her husband, Todd," Frank said. "They're also willing to help, but, of course, you'll have to follow some rules. And trust is earned," he added.

"Yes, sir," I answered. "Will I meet your daughter and her husband?"

"Yes. They're coming down Saturday. Dr. Sue is going to meet with the five of us and we'll establish some expectations for our month together."

We talked for a while, and they explained that they had been talking to Darlene while I was in group therapy.

"Sam?" Frank said as they stood up to leave.

"Yeah, I mean, yes?"

"How far have you progressed in school?"

I paused, feeling my face turn hot.

"As I told you, Sam is smart and learns very quickly," Dr. Sue stated.

I am not a dog!

We left my room and headed toward the living area.

Crap.

There was Eddy and his parents. If I introduced them to him, would they not want me because I came with a boyfriend?

Boyfriend.

I paused. That was the first time I'd even thought of that word.

Is that what he is?

I'd only known him for almost six weeks. Sure, we basically lived together, but ...

"See you Saturday, son," his dad said, giving Eddy a hug.

They walked closer, and there was no way to not introduce them without seeming rude. "Aunt Donna, Uncle Frank, this is Eddy." I motioned toward Eddy and his parents. Eddy introduced his parents and they all shook hands.

"We'll see you Saturday, kid," Frank said.

Donna gave me a hug. When I held my breath and stiffened, Frank and Donna looked uncomfortably at Darlene.

Dr. Sue spoke up quickly. "I told you, she has a lot of work to do. All the physical contact Sam had before she came to this center was abusive."

Eddy's parents followed Aunt Donna and Uncle Frank out the door.

"Great. Now all four of them know," I said with a huff.

"What do they all know?" Eddy asked.

"That I'm damaged."

Eddy's laugh was gentle. "Well, Damaged One, do you wanna play Skip-Bo?"

I nodded.

He sat there shuffling the cards several times, finally he said, "So? How do you feel?"

The cards slipped masterfully between his fingers, then stopped.

I bit my lower lip to try to stop my smile from escaping. "The next month might be all right. If not, Logan will pick me up."

Chapter 13

I felt a cold hand on my face and jumped.

"Shhhhh." Eddy's voice broke the silence of my room.

"Sheesh, you scared the hell out of me," I whispered a little too loudly and looked at my clock. The final bed check was fifteen minutes ago and I hoped no one had heard us.

"I was wondering if you would visit tonight," I said, biting my lower lip.

"Well, actually, if we're going to run, this may be our last chance. I leave tomorrow.," Eddy said. He was on his knees beside my bed, so I leaned up on my elbows to bring us eye to eye.

"I can't ask you to do that," I whispered.

He leaned forward, and I could feel the rhythm of his breathing. "I promised I would go with you."

"I know, but I can't let you throw away everything you have. It wouldn't be right."

He wrapped his arms around me in a big bear hug.

"I don't see it that way," he said, slowly kissing my neck.

I closed my eyes and tried not to think about the fact that I might not ever see him again. He lowered us back onto the bed. I held my breath, glad for the blanket between us.

"But *I* see it that way. You're starting college in the fall to be some kind of brain doctor for kids—"

He kissed me hard and then pulled away abruptly. "And you think me leaving with you tonight would stop me from going to college?"

"I know it will. They'll look for us."

"I'll take you to Logan. In a few months I'll be 18 and I can get a place."

I muffled a laugh. "Thanks, but no. I'll be fine. You go home tomorrow. In a week, I'll go with Donna and Frank."

I gave him a kiss and wiggled my arms out to hug him tight.

"Well, all right," he sighed. "But if you hate it and need to get away, just call me."

"I will, but I don't think I want to run anymore. I want to have a better life. I want to try."

"Okay. They can't live too far from here. Maybe they'll let me see you before you go to Nebraska." He started to kiss me again, and now I wished the blanket was gone. He stopped and pushed up on his hands. I froze. "Not in this place," he groaned, more to himself than to me.

He slid to my side and wrapped his arm around me, glancing at the clock. "I'm going to miss you."

"I'll miss you too," I answered, laying my head on his chest. His heart beat fast.

"I better get going. In about five minutes, Matt's going to have a stomachache again. Unless he falls asleep. We thought I'd need a distraction to get out of the building."

I took a deep breath. "Always thinking ahead?"

"Yep. Are you sure?"

I nodded.

"Okay. I wanna give you something. Promise you won't get mad."

"I don't have anything to give you though."

"I know that. Promise you won't get mad?"

"Okay, I promise."

He handed me a book and gave me a deep kiss before he let go of it. When he heard Matt talking to the night staff, Eddy got up with a groan and ducked out the door.

I waited to hear if the two of them had gotten caught, but the hallway was silent.

The morning sunlight filled my room. I blinked a few times and remembered my new book. I ran my hands through the covers and giggled when I felt it. I rolled it over in my hands. The pages were ruffled, and the brown leather cover was worn. On the bottom corner of the book was printed "Edward P. Pattin, III" in gold lettering.

I laughed to myself. *He is a classic third. Classic!*

I ran my fingers across his name then up to the top of the soft page. *The Holy Bible* was embossed in bold gold letters.

The Bible?

"He didn't!" I said to myself, gritting my teeth.

No wonder he asked me not to get mad.

When I opened the book, a note fell onto the bed. Eddy had written on the inside of the cover.

> Samantha,
> Please don't get mad. I want you to have my Bible.
> I know you aren't happy with God at the moment,
> but it's special to me, so please take good care of it.
> I have told you and shown you how much I love
> you. It's hard for me to admit, but He loves you
> more. Please get to know Him.
>
> > I love you!
> > Eddy

I picked up the piece of paper off my bed and opened it.

Sam,
I highlighted some verses for you. Read them when
you're ready.
His love for you:
John 3:16, page 1381
Ephesians 2:4-5, page 1539

His promise to you:
Romans 10:13, page
1483 Psalms 27:39, page 749
Psalms 27:14, page 741

His sacrifice for you:
Romans 8:3-4, page 1478
John 3:16, page 1381

Call me after you have read them, and I will
explain anything you don't understand. And
remember – you promised not to be mad!

Love,
Eddy

I rolled my eyes, folded the paper back up, and stuck it in the *Bible,* which I set in my top drawer with the necklace from Tara, letter from Logan and photo of my sisters.

I tried not to think about Eddy leaving today as I showered. I slid Logan's shirt over my wet hair and pulled my hair into a ponytail as I headed toward the dining room.

"Where have you been?" Tommy asked.

"Long hot shower. Felt good!" I exclaimed, sitting in my spot.

Eddy slid his foot over mine and I let my leg rest against his. Tommy smirked like he was up to something.

"What's with you?" I asked. Eddy reached across my tray to grab my toast and kissed the top of my head.

"Matt and Tommy have a bet going," Eddy said, taking a bite.

"Oh? And does this bet involve me?" I looked at Tommy.

Matt laughed, "Yep. You and Eddy."

I took another bite of my Cinnamon Life cereal.

Matt whispered something to Tommy.

Eddy shook his head and finished his breakfast before putting his tray away and leaving the dining room.

"So what's the bet?" I asked.

They exchanged winks, shrugged and yelled, "Hey, Eddy, one more game before you go?"

"Okay. Whatever," he yelled back from the TV room.

Tommy, Andy and Matt jumped up to stack the pool balls. The four of them played while Jessica painted my nails, *again*.

Once the game was over, Eddy handed Jessica the pool stick and said, "Matt will teach you how to play, if you want."

She took the stick and said, "Oh, really? Hah! I'll beat their butts."

Eddy sat on the couch next to me and pulled me onto his lap. I wrapped my arms around his neck. We sat quietly for a minute pretending to be interested in an episode of *Seventh Heaven*.

"Are you mad at me?" he murmured.

"No. Why would I be? I mean I'm bummed you're leaving."

He closed his eyes and said, "Please don't avoid my gift."

I gave him a quick kiss on the forehead and said, "I'm not avoiding it and I'm not mad. I'll read it when I'm ready."

He bobbed his head several times. "Please do."

I pulled away to look him in the eyes. "Why? Why is it so important to you?"

He stared for a moment, as if the words he was searching for were hiding deep in my eyes.

"Because I love you." His lips curled into a small smile. "Please read it and keep an open mind."

"I will. I love you, too, Eddy, but I don't ask you to change for me."

His eyes got wide and lips went flat, "I'm not asking you to change. When I asked you if you believed in God your answer was that you didn't know anything about Him. All I am asking is that you get to know Him."

"Fair enough. So, what happens to *us* when you leave?"

He took a deep breath and let it out slowly. "You'll have a phone, so we'll be able to talk. I'm going to ask Donna and Frank if I can come see you. But when you go to Nebraska ... I don't know yet. Maybe when I get to school, I'll visit my counselor to see if there's a college near where you're heading."

When I slid off his lap to the couch, his eyes followed me. "Your parents will flip out," I observed.

"Maybe. But as long as I am going to college and making the grade, they won't have a good reason to stop me."

During family visitation, Eddy's dad carried his son's bags to the car. His mom was signing the discharge papers.

"Can we stay for visitation?" I overheard Eddy ask Jennifer.

She glanced at me and said, "I don't see why not."

Eddy pulled a chair out in front of me in the TV area.

"Eddy told us that your aunt and uncle are coming to visit you today," his mom said, ever cheerful.

"Yes, at least they said they would."

No sign of them, yet.

Eddy reached into his pocket and asked, "Sam, do you know how to use a cell phone?"

I shook my head at the small black device in his hand.

"No problem; it's easy. Turn it on after lights out. I put it on silent mode so no one will hear it ring. I'll try to call you at 10:20; you'll see the screen light up. Press the green button to answer the phone. Press the red button to disconnect. But if you get a roommate, leave it off. Please don't give them any reason to search for this or you'll get in trouble." He pushed the phone into my hand.

"How do I turn it on?" I asked, rolling it over in my palm. Eddy pulled himself to the edge of his seat and took the phone.

His parents were watching him explain how to use the phone, which made me feel pretty stupid.

I wonder what they think about me? I can't be what they want for their son.

Eddy showed me how to turn the phone on and off. He had programmed it so that when I held down the "2," it called his cell.

"Got it?"

"Got it," I answered.

I shoved the phone into my pocket and our eyes met for a minute.

Man, am I going to miss him.

"Samantha?"

My eyes bolted away from his, and I found myself looking up at Aunt Donna, Uncle Frank, a younger couple, and, of course, the ever-present Melanie.

Chapter 14

"This is our daughter, Haley," Donna smiled and pointed to the tall blonde standing next to her.

My eyes met Haley's blue-gray eyes and she shot me a smile. Wearing a pink shirt tucked into belted jeans and pearl earrings that matched her necklace, she appeared well put together, but not flashy. I moved my hand out slowly to shake hers, and she grabbed on and pulled me in for a full-body hug. I stiffened and held my breath, arms limp at my side.

"Oh, please, we won't hurt you," she said, with a laugh. Then pointed to the man next to her. "This is my husband, Todd."

Todd was quiet, keeping his distance as he shook my hand politely. "Nice to meet you, Sam," he said evenly.

The skin around his eyes creased and his mustache waggled when he pursed his lips, as if he was itching to hug me, but understood that Haley's hug was more than enough. Todd was neatly dressed in brown cord shorts and an untucked gray T-shirt, with a blue wave on the back.

"Nice to meet you too. Would you like to sit down?"

Donna and Frank took the couch next to Eddy's parents. They shook hands and started to chat while Haley and Todd found a seat on the other couch. I started to sit in my chair, but Eddy put a hand on my shoulder and pushed me toward Haley and Todd's couch. He took the seat I'd started to sit in, and then he raised his eyebrows, a sly smile sneaking across his face.

"Oh, sorry, Sam. Did you want to sit here?" Eddy said innocently, as he sat back and crossed his foot over one knee.

I scowled. *Shithead!*

"Haley, Todd, this is Eddy and his mom and dad." I gestured toward them. To keep from brushing against Haley, I perched carefully on the corner of the couch.

"Edward. And this is my wife Patty." Dr. Pattin added, getting up and shaking their hands. Haley and Todd both greeted them, then looked at me and Eddy.

I took a deep breath, feeling like I needed to explain why the Pattins were sitting here. "Eddy is my ... best friend, I guess." I hung my head as if I had just admitted to a crime.

Eddy stood up to shake their hands. "I wanted to meet you before we had to leave." Eddy said, "and I'm hoping you'll allow me to see Sam before she goes to Nebraska. May I ask where you live?"

There's that politeness I love in him.

"We have a few acres in Santa Barbara," Haley answered.

"Where do you live?" Todd asked.

"Malibu," Eddy answered with relief in his voice.

"How far is that from Santa Barbara?" I piped up.

"Maybe just an hour," Eddy replied, letting a smile escape.

"They're too young to be so attached. Don't you agree?" Frank asked Eddy's parents.

Shit! Here it comes. They're not going to want a lovesick teenager on their hands.

Eddy's dad broke the awkward silence. "We agree; they *are* young," he paused a moment, then continued, "but we had a talk with Edward, and he is determined to be with Sam. I know my son. I know his soul. If this is the road he wants to travel, nothing will stop him. But he will do it with honor. Correct, son?" He stared hard at Eddy.

"Yes, sir!" Eddy said, his tone strong and clear, almost military.

The room was dead silent for a few minutes, then Haley turned her attention to Eddy and me. "Mom and Dad are picking Sam up next Saturday. What are you planning once she leaves here?"

"Only to talk to each other on the phone for now. Don't want to push my luck," I answered.

Hint, hint, Eddy.

Haley nodded.

"I would like to see Sam on Saturdays, take her to dinner, maybe a movie. Then return her to you," Eddy offered.

I glared at him.

Hello! Didn't you just hear me say I don't want to push my luck?

Todd took a deep breath. "Maybe in a few weeks. Let her get settled. You know she leaves for Nebraska in a month?"

"Nebraska?" his mother-in-law questioned, as if it were some far-off country.

"Dr. Sue said that Sam has been through a lot, so we thought it would be best to keep things simple over the next month," Frank said.

They're planning my life like I couldn't think for myself.

"I don't intend to make things difficult. Just dinner and a movie," Eddy assured them.

"Good enough," Haley said. "We'll see you in two weeks. I'm sure Sam has your number. Once on the ranch, she can call you with ours."

"Thank you," Eddy replied, nodding. He winked at me. "We should leave you guys to chat. Sam? Can I talk to you for a minute?"

I looked at the four people I thought of as my temporary family.

"Do you mind if I say goodbye?"

Eddy grabbed my hand and pulled me out of sight before anyone could answer.

"They seem nice," he mumbled, wrapping his arms around me and squeezing tight.

"I think so," I whispered.

He rested his head on mine and said, "Remember—turn the phone on after final bed check." He pulled back and looked me in the eyes. "Sam, I'll see you in two weeks."

My face got hot when he planted a long hard kiss on me.

"Breathe," he said, resting his forehead against mine. Once my face was back to room temperature, we went back to the families.

Dr. Sue stood waiting for me.

Families were in the middle of Thursday therapy when Dr. Sue called me out. "Sam, we have work to do." She opened the door and let me into her office, where Donna and Frank sat waiting. I took a deep breath, slid into a seat, and focused on my cabin. I barely heard them greet me and I'm not sure if I replied.

What kind of work does Dr. Sue have in mind?

"Sam?" Dr. Sue said.

"Yeah. Sorry. Yes."

"Donna and Frank have a few rules they want to discuss."

I nodded. It wasn't like I had a choice.

"You will go to work with one of us each day. You are not to go anywhere alone," Frank said.

I nodded and bit my lower lip.

Crap.

"No drugs. No smoking. No drinking. No phone calls except with Eddy. But no family contact. We don't want anyone to know where you are."

"Sam, that includes Logan and your sisters," Dr. Sue interrupted.

I closed my eyes tight. My throat knotted and I tried to swallow the hard lump.

"Logan will be told you're in Nebraska, but he can send you letters here and I'll forward them to you. If you want to write him back, mail it to me and I'll forward them. This is a big one, kid. A deal-breaker."

No! I won't see the girls before I leave?

"Okay, I understand kinda, but what about my girls?" I asked, fighting back the burn in my eyes.

What choice do I have?

Before Dr. Sue could answer me, Frank jumped in. "What's the deal with school?" he asked, looking at Dr. Sue.

"Sam can continue home studies until she gets to Nebraska. They'll enroll her in public school there," she answered, as if I wasn't in the room.

"Very good," Frank affirmed.

"Sam, do you want to stay with us under these terms?" Donna asked.

Fine—it's only for one month, then I'm out of there. I don't really want anything to do with Stacy's family.

"Yes," I whispered.

"We plan to pick you up Saturday before lunch. It's a long ride and we want to get home before dark. Will that work, Dr. Sue?" Frank asked.

"Yes. That's fine. She'll be ready. You know she doesn't have much to take?"

"Yes. As we said, we'll get her proper clothing, shoes, and whatever else Sam will need for Nebraska. That's not a concern," Donna said, and finally addressed me. "Do you like to read, Sam?"

Dr. Sue was standing in front of my cabin, so I was staring blankly at three red books on the middle shelf of a bookshelf across the room. I nodded.

"I'll have her ticket to Boys Town before you pick her up. Can you handle taking her to the airport?"

"Yes," Frank and Donna answered, almost together.

"Okay. Samantha, you need to sign this contract. It simply says that you agree to follow all the rules explained here tonight."

I picked up the blue pen and set it on the page. Above the line I was to sign, it read: "If Samantha breaks even one of the above rules, she will be returned temporarily to New Life Treatment Center and then taken to San Diego Juvenile Detention Center."

Yikes, juvie! What if I mess up accidentally?

The pen scratched as I signed *Samantha Rain* on the line. Donna, Frank and Dr. Sue scribbled their names below mine.

After Donna and Frank left, Dr. Sue asked me how I was doing. Even though I nodded, she asked again. That knot in my throat felt as big as a baseball and my face felt as if all the blood had drained from it. When a tear escaped from my eye, I wiped it away, annoyed that it had dared to sneak out.

"Sam? Talk to me. I do get that this is hard for you. I might be able to help."

I shook my head, willing the tears to stop, and looked at my copy of the contract.

"I'm just tired," I choked out.

And disappointed that I won't see my sisters!

The lump was now the size of a big grapefruit and growing bigger by the second, making it hard to breathe.

"I'll be here Saturday to see you off if you decide you want to talk. I'll tell the staff it's alright if you want to stay in your room the rest of this evening," she said. She spoke tenderly, a sadness to her voice.

I nodded and whispered, "Sure. I'll get ready for bed."

"They'll do normal bed check," she warned.

"Yeah, I know. See you Saturday." With that, I bolted out and hurried to my room. The floodgate was getting ready to break and I had no idea how to handle this feeling.

The fading sunlight was shining through the blinds. I pulled on the T-shirt Eddy gave me, twisted the blinds shut and curled up under the covers.

I had spent all week going through my normal routine. Class, art, music, group therapy, Skip-Bo with Jessica and Shannon. I even accepted a challenge from the boys to play pool. No surprise, they creamed me. I gave the appearance that I was fine. That I was not worried about Saturday. That I didn't miss Eddy and that I wasn't afraid that he wouldn't miss me. But I was scared.

Can't go anywhere alone? Shit! Are they planning to tie me to my bed each night? What about the bathroom? Will one of them watch me pee, too? Stop it, Sam! You're acting insane.

I let the tears flow onto my pillow.

The door creaked open and Melanie peeked her head in. She said gently, "Sam? Dr. Sue asked us to let you know that the families have left."

My voice came out hushed and hoarse. "Thanks." When I didn't budge, the door clicked shut again.

I was afraid I'd never see my sisters or Logan again. The floodgates flew open once more and I closed my eyes and cried. My body got heavy.

Suddenly, a chill ran down my spine. Heavy footsteps pounded out in the hallway. As they got closer, the hair on the back of my neck prickled. Someone was in my room! They stopped beside my bed and a hand grabbed my shoulder.

I shot up and looked around. No one.

Oh, it must have been one of my dreams.

Just then, the screen on my phone lit up green. I tried to take a deep breath and felt the sting in my lungs. If I answered, he'd know I'd been crying. The screen stopped glowing and I dropped back onto the bed.

Damn. I need to hear his voice.

After a few minutes, I picked up my phone. Like magic, it lit up. A smile snuck across my face.

"Hello," I whispered, not sure if they were watching me closer than normal tonight.

Eddy laughed. "Ahh, Baby, I was afraid I wouldn't get to talk to you tonight."

Chapter 15

I wished I hadn't eaten breakfast. My stomach felt like I had drunk sour milk.

Jennifer sat on my bed watching me pack stuff from my top drawer in the red duffel bag Melanie had brought. I zipped up the bag and slung the long handle over my shoulder.

I froze when I saw Donna standing at the staff station with Melanie and Dr. Sue. They were looking through a stack of papers, discussing each one, and then slipping it into a manila folder.

"So, this says her birthday was a few weeks ago. Did anyone—?" Donna asked.

"No." Melanie said.

Dr. Sue cleared her throat and they both looked up. Frank, who had been sitting on the other side of the station, was by my side before I could blink.

"Are you ready?"

I nodded, wishing I knew where I was going.

"Donna has your ticket to Nebraska—you leave in 35 days. Do as you're told, Sam. Think of this as a fresh start," Melanie said kindly.

"A clean slate, huh?" I grumbled and followed them out the front doors. The heavy double doors shut with the same click that trapped me there seven weeks ago. This time I was leaving, so why didn't I feel free?

Frank reached for my bag as we walked toward their white SUV. I flinched and said, "It's not heavy."

He opened the back door for me. Before getting in, I glanced back at the cream-colored stucco building. Both

Dr. Sue and Melanie stood on the front porch and waved. Above them loomed the blue-and-white sign: *New Life Treatment Center—a Center for Problem Adolescents.*

I bit my lip and swallowed back the vomit coming up my throat.

Did I have a problem? Or was I the problem?

I climbed into the backseat and tossed the duffel bag next to me. Donna turned around and reached out to hand me something.

"Jennifer said this is yours."

My camera. "Yes. Thanks."

I tried not to smile, afraid that if they knew it was special to me, they'd find a reason to take it away. I unzipped my bag just enough to slip it inside.

I sat silent in the back as they drove up the 101 Highway.

Does anyone even know where these people are taking me? Maybe this isn't such a good idea after all.

I saw the sign: *101 North.*

The ocean view spanned my window, and I tried to lose myself in the never-ending water. A few surfers were sitting on boards out past the waves, reminding me of Jeff. I wondered how he was doing, if maybe he was out there now.

We drove for what felt like hours. We drove in the opposite direction from where my sisters lived.

There was a football game on the radio, and I wished they had turned on music instead.

Ventura.

After a few hours we stopped for food. Frank asked if I needed to use the ladies' room. I shook my head, and he pulled into the drive-through line.

"Are we getting out?" I asked, hoping to stretch my legs and get my phone out of the pocket of the jeans in my bag.

"No. Sam, I'll be honest with you. Melanie and Dr. Sue are afraid that if we let you out of the car before we get home, you'll run away." Donna said apologetically, glancing back at me.

My eyes opened wide and my jaw dropped.

"Are you hungry?" Frank asked.

"No," I said flatly. Frank ordered food and we got back on the road.

101 North

Frank ate while he drove. Then, finally, we exited the 101.

State Street.

I glanced at the clock; we had left the center four hours ago.

"Are we close?" I asked.

It's getting dark.

"About an hour away." Donna said.

Fairgrounds on the right. I'm not going to remember this.

That last hour seemed to take forever. One open green field after another. Horses. More horses. Houses like I'd never seen before. Barns that were nicer than my mother's house. It got dark, very dark ... we made a right but it was too dark to see a street sign. Was there one?

Finally, we stopped in front of a big black metal gate.

I knew it. They're going to lock me up in this place. That's it. I'm calling Eddy to come pick me up. ASAP!

I watched as Frank pushed a button on a garage door opener attached to his car's visor. The gate split and we drove inside. Then it closed behind us.

I frowned.

When Eddy comes, I'll have to figure out how to get through the gate. I don't have one of those clicker things.

Gravel crunched under our tires. Headlights shined on red rose bushes in front of white wood fences then darkness.

Oh, Wow! I looked up and saw thousands of stars!

"This is the orchard," Donna said as we reached a Y and went right. Just when I decided I could climb the gate, I heard barking. A lot of barking.

Dogs.

My eyes darted to the left side of the house, then to the fruit trees. Frank brought the car to a stop and got out. Five dogs came running from the house.

My palms started to sweat.

No! If I try to give them the slip, one of these dogs will hear me. Damn!

"They won't bite you. Come on out," Donna urged. She got out of the car and greeted each dog with, "Yes, we're home. Good dog!"

Wagging tails or not, all I saw was a pack of white teeth. I reached for the door handle and paused. I had sat so long that I was worried my legs wouldn't work if I had to run.

"Come on," Donna said, opening my door.

I hesitated, then grabbed my bag. Five little noses touched my legs before I stepped on the gravel.

I looked down and slowly tapped the biggest one between his floppy ears.

"That's Spike," Donna said amiably, walking toward a cute little white house. I studied it as we walked. It reminded me of the cabin picture in Dr. Sue's office. Three black and gray spotted dogs followed her.

"How can you tell them apart? They all look the same, except the bigger one," I asked, pulling my bag over my shoulder and picking up the pace to catch up.

"They're all from the same litter. Well, except this one." She pointed to a little one next to her. "She's the little mother."

Her voice was soft, loving.

It's hard to believe she's related to my mom.

"This is Haley and Todd's house. You're going to stay with them. Haley will be home soon; she had to cover my shift today," she explained.

The word *home* echoed in my mind.

We walked through the backdoor of the house and into a bright white kitchen. I stopped walking, The house was small and cozy. I ran my hand over the white tile island. From the kitchen, you could see the French-style glass front door. Next to the front door was a huge picture window.

Was there a lake outside that window?

Under the window was a dark denim couch, with red pillows on it. The large wooden-rectangular kitchen table was in between the living room and kitchen. A few paintings of horses or the ocean hung on each wall. I watched as Donna walked between the island and kitchen sink to an open door.

"This will be your room," she stated, snapping me back into motion. In the middle of the room was a big neatly-made bed with a purple-and-blue plaid comforter. The pillows had running horses on them.

My room?

I set my bag on the bed and scanned it. On both sides of the bed was a window with curtains made from the same horse fabric as the pillows.

They must really like horses.

Donna clicked on a lamp next to the bed and opened a door across from the bed.

"Sam, here's the closet, Haley got it all cleaned out for you. That door leads to your bathroom," Donna pointed.

My bathroom? Oh, jeez!

"You can unpack with Haley later. Want to help me feed the dogs, then see my house?"

She walked out of the room and I followed. Directly across from my room was another door.

"That's Haley and Todd's room. They'll show you around tomorrow"

She picked up three dog bowls and the three dogs came to sit in the kitchen. I watched her toss some kibble into each one, then poured some warm water over it. I had a moment to look at the dogs better and they didn't all look alike. Spike was the biggest with floppy ears and a black mask over his eyes.

The dogs watched every move Donna made as she set each bowl back onto the floor and said their names: "Spike. Kanga. Cricket."

I watched their ears. The other two had ears that stood up and one had a mask like Spike's, while the other only had one eye covered. *They were cute!*

I followed her out of the house in silence. Lights clicked on and we walked through an open lattice gate. We walked along a big pool framed with bricks. Beyond the pool were bushes and trees trapped in by a lattice fence.

"If we're having company, we close these gates and keep the dogs in here," Donna explained as she walked.

"This is our house."

We walked up four stairs to a little landing with a built-in grill. A water fountain in the shape of a horse head hung on the wall. The slow, steady stream of water flowing from the horse's mouth reminded me that I needed to pee. Four more stairs took us to a big covered deck. When I turned left, I faced a wall of windows, with a French door in the middle.

Donna opened the door and motioned for me to go in. Across the huge room, Frank, stretched out in a big leather recliner, watching football on the TV. Two couches filled the corner beyond him. To the right sat a round oak table with four chairs and to my left was a kitchen. It was all one huge room.

"That door leads to our bedroom and bathroom." Donna gestured across the room. "Would you like something to drink?"

I shook my head and looked around. Draft horse photos lined one wall. The last two of the five dogs were sleeping on the denim couch that was covered with a blanket.

I took a deep breath and turned to see Donna standing at the large kitchen island, cute little cow or chicken kitchen items on the counter.

"I'm going to feed my dogs. Once Haley gets home, we planned to go to dinner." She turned and opened a floor-length cupboard. Both dogs jumped off the couch and sat in the kitchen.

"Oh, and this is Daisy and Cece," Donna stated. She must have seen me watching them.

"What kinda dogs are they?"

"Heelers, working dogs," Donna smiled.

She loves her dogs.

We went and sat on the deck and waited for Haley. I looked out across the deck, across the pool, and to Haley and Todd's house.

Wow! They must sit out here for hours.

"Frank's birds, greenhouse and chickens are over there." Donna pointed down a little brick path that ran along their house. Darkness filled the rest.

Before my eyes could adjust, all five dogs bolted down the steps and went into full guard-dog bark. They ran out the open gate and onto the gravel driveway. The sound of tires on the gravel hit my ears before I saw the headlights.

"That's Haley. I'm going to freshen up. See you in a few minutes for dinner."

"Cuz? You here?" Haley yelled.

I looked at Donna, feeling a bit lost, but she simply grinned and went back up the deck steps. I walked toward the little white house, peeking around the open gate to see if any dogs were coming.

"Yes, I'm here," I called out. Haley had on a full-length dress with busy bracelets that clinked on her wrist. She waited for me in front of the door to her house. When she grabbed me into another one of her hugs, I stiffened like a board. In a lame attempt to return her gesture, I tapped her back twice with my hand.

Finally releasing me, she asked, "Did you get settled? All unpacked?"

"No, Donna told me to wait for you. But I don't have much, so it won't take long."

We went inside, she sat cross legged on the bed, and I dumped my stuff out next to her.

"This is all you have?" she asked, pointing to the pile in front of her.

"Yes, sorry," I said.

She gave me a sideways look. "Not your fault. We'll get you what you need on Monday. I have the day off and *we are going shopping!*" She held up my obviously-handmade wood-bead necklace and looked at it like it was a worm.

"My friend gave it to me."

"Hmmm." She set it on the nightstand and picked up Eddy's Bible.

"Eddy gave it to me. He said I should get to know God."

"I might like that boy after all. Did he suggest what parts you should read first? The Bible can be confusing."

I swallowed hard. "Kinda. There's a note. I haven't read anything yet."

As she looked over the note, her lips straightened, and her eyebrows almost touched.

"His note says that you're mad at God. How come?"

I took a deep breath and exhaled slowly. "Eddy says that God has a plan for me. I told him that if God put me here on purpose, then I don't think I want to know Him."

Haley studied Eddy's unopened Bible. "I understand, but I agree with Eddy. God does have a plan for you. So, Sam, this is all you have?"

"Yep."

"Okay, then. Well, we're all leaving in fifteen minutes to meet Todd for dinner."

She left the room, and I shoved the picture of my sisters in the frame of the mirror above the dresser. I picked up my jeans and pulled out Eddy's phone from the pocket. It was still off. I set it next to Tara's necklace and put my shirts in the top drawer of the dresser. Then I sat on the bed and turned on my phone.

Just as the screen turned green, Frank yelled, "Sammie! ... Let's roll!"

Sighing, I tossed the phone into the nightstand drawer.

Chapter 16

The smell of fresh-baked bread with, maybe, rosemary? filled the street and made my stomach groan.

I stood behind Haley while the hostess showed us to our table. The restaurant was dimly lit with sconces lining the tan walls and candles at each table. I could see enough to know that I was out of place.

"Is Todd coming?" I asked, taking my seat and running my hand over the ironed white tablecloth.

Donna leaned over and whispered, "He's here."

Where?

I glanced around the packed room. Tables were full of people talking, laughing and eating.

Haley pointed to the menu in front of me and said, "What do you want for dinner?" I opened it and froze.

Oh, shit.

I had never been in a restaurant before. In fact, I had never ordered from a menu. A bead of sweat trickled down my forehead.

"Sam? Do you like chicken, fish, pork or beef?" Haley asked, taking a sip of her ice water.

"Chicken?" I said, like I was hoping *chicken* was the right answer.

"Well, then, we'll ask Todd to make you something with chicken. Wait and see ... he'll dazzle you." She smiled with pride and handed her menu to the waitress, telling her what we wanted.

Donna and Frank ordered "the usual," to share.

I was totally confused. *Where* was Todd?

A minute later he appeared wearing khakis with a gray button-up shirt and green tie. He stopped at a few tables and talked to the patrons before sitting next to Haley.

"Well Sam, it's great to have you with us. Chicken, huh?" Todd repeated, a smile slipping out from under his mustache.

"Yes. Please. Are you the cook?" I asked.

"The cook, the zookeeper, depends on the night." He grinned, giving Haley a quick kiss and standing up. "See you in a bit." He stopped at a few tables to shake hands and smile, then disappeared behind a swinging door.

"Does he work here every night?" I asked.

"Yes. It's his baby. Todd ... well, *we* own this place," Haley answered, dipping a piece of bread in oil and popping it into her mouth.

Wow! I had never been to a restaurant and here they owned one.

When our meals were served, Todd joined us. They all talked about the day. Of course, I had nothing to add. Actually, I was stunned and silent. I had never tasted anything like this.

The chicken with lemon sauce melted in my mouth, the hint-of-garlic mashed potatoes were creamy. No way was this meal from a box or freezer I tried to eat slowly and take small bites.

Damn, it was too good.

Donna and Frank headed to their house. Haley gave me a quick hug in the kitchen, then went to her room. I stood frozen for a minute before going to mine.

I guess I'm going to have to get used to these hugs.

I changed into Eddy's T-shirt and grabbed the Ziploc bag that held my travel-sized toothbrush and toothpaste. Then I flipped on the light in the bathroom and stopped cold. A stack of soft blue towels was neatly folded on a bench next to a white-tiled shower, framed with glass.

No shower curtain, just glass.

I walked over to the sink. There was a pink-flower-shaped bar of soap, a toothbrush and toothpaste all still in their packages sitting on a marble vanity. Haley had propped a note on them that read, "Welcome, Sam."

I had only seen a toothbrush like this on commercials and at the grocery store. The bristles were different colors, with some taller than others. It felt funny when I brushed with it.

I took my time washing my face, studying myself in the mirror. Not just myself, but the reflection of me in this beautiful bathroom. It looked like something in a magazine. I couldn't believe that people really lived like this.

A knot formed in my throat as I climbed into the big soft bed.

I had never called Eddy—he always called me, but I needed to hear his voice. I pulled the phone out of the nightstand, grabbed a pillow and hugged it tightly as I held down the "2" button.

"Sam? Are you okay?" Eddy asked, answering instantly, and my wet cheeks blushed hot red. I loved that voice.

"Yes. I'm fine," I whispered, afraid Haley would hear me.

"I was worried. I'm so glad you're okay. Hey, I'm at practice. Can I call you back?" he said, sounding distracted.

"You don't have to. I just wanted to hear your voice. Sorry to bother you," I said, worried that he was mad that I'd called. But I wanted to tell him about today.

"You? Bother me? Sam. Never. I've been waiting for you to call. I'll call you back at 11. Good?"

Phew!

"Uh-huh. Eddy, I love you."

He paused and grumbled, "I'm coming!" to someone in the background.

"Good. But just so you know: I love you more. Sam. I gotta go. Coach's vein is starting to pop out of his neck." He laughed and hung up.

I set the phone back on the nightstand. It was quiet, nothing but crickets.

Crap! I have never said, "I love you" first. What a day! My sisters should see this place! Eddy has a coach?

My mind wouldn't stop buzzing. A cool tear crept down my cheek and slid to the pillow. I closed my eyes just as my body got warm and heavy.

Footsteps were pounding, getting closer. I squeezed my eyes tight, and my heart raced faster than two Jack Russell's chasing a chicken. The door creaked open, and a hand grabbed my shoulder. My whole body flung away from the touch.

"NO!" I screamed, sitting up straight.

Where am I?

I wiped the sweat off my forehead and looked around the bright sunlit room.

Oh, wow. I'm at the ranch. I'm okay. I'm okay.

There were voices outside, and I looked at the alarm clock. "10 am? I slept so late! Oh, how rude," I said to the empty room as I jumped out of bed.

I checked my phone: two missed calls and one text message.

A text message? Shit. I better ask Eddy how to use this phone. Later.

My teeth were brushed and I was dressed in record time.

"Hello," I said, peeking out the doorway.

No answer. The house was empty, so I went through the kitchen and out the back door. Then stopped. Spike greeted me and I petted him as I looked around. To the right, the sun was on the top of the orchard and sprinklers misted the tree trunks. To the left was that water tower, higher than the houses. I noticed steps on the side of it.

I'll check that out later.

I could hear voices to the left, so I went that way. Spike and I walked past the orchard. In the middle of the driveway was a single tree.

A huge tree.

I walked over and put my hand on it. It had to be twenty feet around, full of green leaves and taller than the barn next to it. I leaned against the tree to stare at the old white barn with green trim. The door was slid open enough that I could see a very big, partially covered wagon inside and a loft above it. I wondered what was in the loft. I took a few steps toward the barn.

My eyes narrowed, and I spotted another little white building to the right of the barn. It had five doors marked with green "*X*s" on the side, facing the houses.

"What is that?" I asked Spike, who was sitting next to me. He tilted his head when I spoke. When I took a step toward the building, he did too.

That's too big to be a doghouse. If it is a doghouse, man, they must really love these dogs!

Directly across from the barn was a huge sandbox scattered with big wooden boxes and what looked like freestanding fences. Haley was in the sandbox riding a big brown horse. I watched as his black tail flowed behind him.

I thought I had finally figured out the layout. The ranch was a square, framed by white fencing. The huge tree was right in the middle. I backed up to the tree to

watch Haley, then hesitantly walked over to the fence. I
had seen a horse only once before when Logan's dad took
us to the racetrack.

I remembered that day. We hadn't sat in the stands
with the crowd. Logan and I carried backpacks and sat
outside the stables while his dad talked to some friends.
The horses were being brushed and washed. They were
beautiful! But it was nothing like watching this.

I crossed my arms on top of the fence and rested my
chin on them. Haley and the horse glided as if they were
one. She sat on top, barely moving, as the horse circled the
objects in the sandbox. Then Haley and her horse ran up
to one of the boxes and jumped over it. *What!*

A loud bang behind me made me jump and spin
around. Todd had dropped an empty wheelbarrow. He
looked different in jeans, a T-shirt and rubber boots.

"Well, good morning, sleepyhead!" he declared,
coming to stand next to me. I bit my lower lip to stop a
nervous smile.

*Is this breaking the rules? Coming out here without
one of them? Well, Spike's here.*

I glanced down to make sure my partner in crime was
still with me. He was.

Todd's calm face assured me that I was not in trouble.

"Sorry about sleeping in. I don't know what happened.
That bed is so comfortable."

He put his hands on his hips and said, "Are you
hungry?"

"No, thanks," I said, looking back at the horse as he
glided over one of the fences.

WOW!

"Well, Mike has pancakes for you. I have to get to
work." Todd walked toward the house, one of the dogs
close behind him. I could hear him talking to the little dog.
The dog's tail was wagging like crazy. "Is that Kanga or
Cricket?" I asked Spike and he laid down.

Mike? Who's Mike? Now another person...

I turned back to watch Haley, who was just walking the horse around now. She had the rope to his mouth loose now and one hand on her hip as they just walked around a few times.

The calming aroma of coffee filled the air. Donna had appeared out of nowhere and was standing next to me with a cow-print mug in her hand.

"Did you eat?" she asked.

"No, but Todd said someone named Mike is saving me pancakes."

She laughed. "Todd names everything. Mike is the microwave. Jenn is the oven. Mike and Jenn Air. Sam, I took today off, just in case you needed me here." She patted my shoulder.

Haley jumped off her horse and walked out of the sandbox. The horse's head bobbed and swung side to side behind Haley, as his feet clinked and flung rocks. This horse was much taller than me.

Haley tied him to the building and said, "Did you sleep well?" as she started to un-Velcro the braces on his lower legs.

"Yes. Sorry I slept so late. I didn't mean to be rude." She gave the horse a pat on the shoulder and pulled up on straps that held the saddle on.

"We figured you needed the sleep. This is Abner." She motioned to the massive animal standing in front of me and pulled the saddle off his back.

"He's beautiful!"

I reached up slowly to touch him, then quickly dropped my hand to my side. He turned his neck and glared at me with big dark-brown eyes, like I had something he wanted.

My arm, no doubt.

"What?" I said to the horse, shoving my hands in my pockets.

Haley stifled a giggle. "He wants a carrot. They're behind you in that box."

She picked up his foot and scraped it with a metal thing.

Ouch!

I turned around and, sure enough, a giant bag of carrots sat next to odd-looking brushes inside a box. I picked up a carrot and shoved it toward Haley.

"You can give it to him," she urged.

My eyes got wide and I pulled the carrot back.

Haley set his leg down and said, "Break it in half and put your hand out like a plate. He'll take it off your hand." She went to his other side and picked up the third foot.

I took a deep breath and slowly walked over to this mammoth. He stretched out his neck and sniffed my pocket. I stiffened.

Here goes nothing!

The carrot made a snapping sound when I broke it, and Abner's ears shot up. I put my hand out flat, balancing the carrot on it, then moved it in front of his nose. I was more than aware he had teeth in there, and from the size of his head, those teeth had to be big. His lips pursed out and moved across my hand. I held my breath. He took the carrot with his lips, like a kid who knew he'd get in trouble for snatching a cookie.

A huge smile lit up my face. I think I even giggled. He strained his neck back out for the other half. This time I stepped closer to him; he was not so intimidating after all.

"I have to go to work for a few hours. Wanna come with me or stay home with mom?" Haley asked.

Mom? Oh yes. Donna is Haley's mom. DUH!

I watched Abner chew. "I'll go with you. Is Donna good with that? She said she took the day off."

"She's fine. She works a lot so staying home is good for her. I need to rinse him off and put him away then shower. You can shower first." She turned on a hose and started to rinse him off. I took that as my cue to get moving.

Spike followed me to the house, and when I got out of the shower, he was asleep on my bed. When I asked him if he was allowed up there, his eyes glanced up, but his head didn't move. I decided he really *was* cute. Once dressed and ready, I picked up my phone.

Text message. Hmm. View Now ... Okay.

"I'm hoping you're asleep. I'll turn on your ringer and set up voicemail when I see you. Hit Reply to answer this. Oh, and I love you."

Reply? Oh, I see it.

I typed "I Can't wait to see you. Love you too."

"Sam. Ready?" Haley yelled from the kitchen.

"Yes!" *Oh, how do I send this? Hmmm, this button worked before so ...*

"Message Sent."

Chapter 17

"We won't be here long. I need to check in," Haley explained, as she led the way across the courtyard toward a surf shop. "Plus, I can't take you shopping tomorrow dressed like that."

I pulled at the bottom of Logan's faded-black Metallica T-shirt. Next to Haley, with her perfect-fitting, pink-flowered capris and white button-up shirt, I was suddenly conscious of my oversized jeans with holes across the knees.

Man, do I always look this bad?

We walked into a store and Haley clunked her purse down on the glass counter where a pretty blonde behind the counter promptly picked it up and shoved it under the cash register. The wood floors looked like they were cut from driftwood and then clear coated. Along one wall, brightly-colored surfboards stood vertically in a row, lined up according to size.

I ran my hand from the tallest board to the smallest one. Skateboards and rollerblades filled shelves covering the adjacent wall. Rows of wheels packaged in bags and hanging from hooks separated the skateboards from the roller blades.

Haley sparked up a conversation with a few kids who were playing on a surf simulator. When she noticed me approaching, she announced, "Okay, Sam, let's get to work." She spun around and marched to the middle of the store, straightening piles of clothes on the way.

"Sam, you are a winter."

I raised my eyebrows. "A winter?"

"Yes, look!" Haley said, pointing.

"Your pure white skin, blue eyes, and dark brown hair means you would look best in winter colors."

My forehead creased and I bit my bottom lip.

What the hell does that mean?

"Sam. Do you understand the color wheel?" Haley asked.

I shook my head.

I'm not stupid, but what the heck's a color wheel?

"Okay, stay here a moment."

I watched her reflection in the mirror as she walked away and then caught sight of my own reflection.

Man, my hair is bad, my clothes are horrible and my shoes hurt my feet. I don't belong here!

I wanted to disappear.

She came back and shoved a pink shirt under my chin.

"This is a spring color. It's not for you. You can wear it if you love pink, but it washes you out." Haley said, tossing the shirt onto the counter and shoving a blue shirt under my chin.

"This is a winter color. It makes your eyes pop and your skin glow. Good color for you. See the difference?"

"Yes," I replied. And I did.

"So I want you to pick out two shirts, a T-shirt and a nicer shirt, like a Polo or a button-up."

"But I don't have any mon—"

"I know. We told you we would get you what you need to go to Nebraska. Now bring me two shirts. Good afternoon, Mrs. West," she said, turning abruptly and heading over to talk to a blonde lady.

I took a deep breath and turned to face the sea of clothing.

I had never seen a store like this. I mean, at the Goodwill, everything is by size, so you find your size and then look for something you want to wear.

This was different. Clothing was arranged by style, then size. I found some blue shirts and held one up to see if I liked it.

"Sorry, Sam. I meant to show you around, but Mrs. West came in. The right side of the store is boys and menswear. The left side, girls and women's."

"Where do you want me to pick from?"

She smiled and waved her arms from one side of the store to the other. "If you like something, bring it to me. I will explain if it's right for you or not."

I scanned the girls' section and found a teal-blue button-up shirt. I pulled it out and held it at arm's length. Then I tucked it under my arm.

Now a T-shirt. Maybe from the other side of the store.

After what seemed like forever, I found Haley talking to some guys about a surfboard. She excused herself and took the shirts from me.

"Good colors for you. Go try them on; we need to figure out your correct size too."

When I came out of the dressing room, she giggled and handed me the same shirts in a smaller size.

"What size did you try on? Extra-extra-large? You can actually wear a medium, but you're used to big clothes, so we'll start with large," she sighed.

When I came out in the form-fitting button-up shirt over my two-sizes-too-big pants held up with a belt, Haley smiled.

"Beautiful. This shirt is great because you can button it like you have it now. Or leave it open with a little camisole under it," she paused, then continued. "This part is going to be more challenging. Jeans! Come on."

I followed her back to the ladies' area. "Jeans come in sizes and styles. Fitted. Relaxed. Slim. Bootcut. What do you like?"

How would I know? Mostly I wear secondhand sweatpants, but I'm not telling her that!

I shrugged.

Haley looked me up and down, and then said, "Well, try all of these. I wanna see them on you."

After I decided on the loose-fit boot-cut legs, she sent me to look at shoes.

Beneath and on each side of the huge front window were shoe racks. I picked up a pair of black Vans.

"What size?" she asked.

I just looked at her.

She shook her head. "Right. Okay. Put your foot on this." She nudged a foot measurer toward me with the toe of her shoe. The shoes she picked out felt amazing.

Haley looked at my old shoes and said, "Who drew these signs on them?" I shrugged.

She tossed them in the trash with a loud bang.

"Don't draw on your clothes," she said, taking all the tags off the new jeans and shirts. She tossed the T-shirt and jeans at me.

"Go change."

I came out of the dressing room just in time to see Logan's shirt fly into the trash. I gasped.

"No!"

Haley pulled it out and held it up. "Sam, it's ugly. It has holes in it, and it's too big."

"It's my brother's."

She took a deep breath and exhaled slowly.

"Is the one you had on yesterday his too?"

"No. Eddy's." I stared at my new shoes and fidgeted.

"Okay. You can keep those two shirts to sleep in or wear on the ranch. But everything else goes in the trash. Deal?"

I nodded.

At the grocery store, Haley smelled the fruit and veggies. She got a box of cereal without looking at the store-brand options. No coupons. And the only frozen item was the tiniest carton of ice cream I'd ever seen. Ben and Jerry's Chubby Hubby.

Chubby Hubby?

"Sam? Do you need any personal items?"

"Not yet," I answered.

She wasn't even using a cart. Just a little basket.

"Well, why don't you pick out some shampoo?"

I looked for the cheapest and handed it to her.

"*This* one smells the best to you?"

I laughed. "Umm. I didn't smell it."

Haley popped the lid and took a whiff, then shoved it in my face. She pulled a few more off the shelf, and we smelled them until my eyebrows raised. That bottle went into her basket.

We got home before Todd and I helped carry things in. I wanted to go through the bag of clothes on my bed, but instead I went to help Haley. She was washing grapes when I walked into the kitchen. From the looks of the refrigerator and cupboards, they went to the grocery store a lot.

"Hell-o-o? Haley, you home?" an unfamiliar voice yelled.

"Come in," she yelled back.

I bolted past Haley to the safety of my room

"We saw your car. Where's Todd? Oh, I'll bet he's checking in at work. So, did your little cousin get here? Where is she? I want to meet her!"

I heard Haley laugh. Was she thinking the same thing I was?

That woman was really peppy!

I snickered and peeked around the door frame. There stood this blonde woman wearing cream-colored linen overalls, a white shirt and a huge white sunhat. Haley motioned me into the room. "Sam, this is my friend and neighbor, Anne. And her husband, Rick."

"Nice to meet you." I hung on the kitchen island.

Anne flew the three steps across the kitchen and hugged me. I tried to slide backwards, but she held tight. All I could do was hold my breath and pray she'd let go.

Finally, she leaned back and took both of my hands, extending my arms to look me over. "Oh, Haley. She is adorable! Something will have to be done about this hair. But so much potential."

Hey! I'm standing right here!

Anne continued as if I couldn't hear her. "I love her skin. You cannot go in the sun! Her skin is perfect."

She let me go and sat at the island next to her husband. Rick didn't say a word as he pushed back his dark hair, then smoothed out his mustache.

"Todd is making chicken tacos for dinner. Wanna stay?" Haley asked.

"Yes! We'll get dessert. Rick, do you mind if we run to the store?"

"Any requests?" Rick asked. As he stood up, I noticed that he was taller than Todd. He was wearing jeans and a tan-colored turtleneck, even though it wasn't cold outside.

Bet he avoids the sun, too.

"This is her first day here—we have to celebrate!" Anne said in a bright voice.

Haley laughed loudly. "You know I don't need an excuse for dessert."

I stepped backwards slowly to my room.

Phew!

I put the clothes away and looked at a book about horses until Haley knocked on my door.

"Sam? Do you wanna help me feed the dogs?"

"Sure." I jumped up.

She had changed into sweatpants and a T-shirt. "In that bench are three bowls. Let me warn you, my dogs will hear the lid of that bench close and be by your side in a heartbeat."

There was a white bench under the kitchen window. I lifted the lid, took a deep breath and pulled out the bowls, trying to close the lid quietly. She was right. Before the food was in the bowls, three of the dogs appeared. Sitting. Staring. Waiting.

"Spike you know. The middle one is Kanga, and the little one is Cricket. The other two, Cece and Daisy, are Mom's," Haley said, as she set the bowls on the floor.

"And Cricket is their mom?" I asked. I know Donna already explained this to me, but it gave me something to talk to Haley about.

"Yep. All four are hers."

"Oh. Can I help you start dinner?"

"Nope, Todd cooks. I clean up afterwards."

"But he cooks every night at work. Maybe he wants us to cook for him. I can cook. Kinda."

"Oh, Sam—that's kind of you. But Todd loves to cook. I love my store. We both like what we do," Haley explained.

Todd came home, turned on the Dan Fogelberg, and started pulling vegetables out of the refrigerator. Apparently Frank and Donna were joining us because Frank popped his head in to ask how long until dinner. Haley followed Frank out to feed the horses. I stayed to help Todd, although he didn't seem to need or want help.

Todd picked up every piece of produce and sniffed it, closing his eyes to take in the smell. He cut and diced to perfection. He masterfully poured olive oil in a frying pan and, once it was warm, placed chicken in it and sprinkled the pieces with a little pepper and herbs. Waving his hand to draw the steam toward his face, he breathed in deeply. Even though he was buzzing around, he looked at peace.

Anne came bouncing into the kitchen, announcing triumphantly. "We found blackberry cobbler."

Rick followed her and added, "And vanilla ice cream."

Anne, Haley, Rick and I sat at the island and visited. Todd continued to cook while chitchatting. When dinner was ready, Haley pushed a button on the wall and declared, "Dinner is ready!"

What was that?

A minute later, Donna and Frank came in the back door, two dogs at their feet. We all sat at the long wood table. They all reached out and took hands. I hesitated, looking at Anne's hand to my right and Haley's to my left. They were both waiting for mine. I took a deep breath, wiped my hands on my pants and limply set mine in theirs.

Donna was sitting across from me and must have seen my confusion. She leaned toward me and murmured, "We give thanks for all we have."

Frank began to pray. As soon as the last word slipped from his mouth, I pulled my hands out of Haley's and Anne's firm grasp.

Todd's chicken tacos were a masterpiece. I wondered how these people didn't all weigh 300 pounds! I enjoyed every bite, completely forgetting Anne and Rick's cobbler was next. But I managed to eat a small bit—and it was amazing!

Donna and Frank went to bed after dessert. I offered to load the dishwasher so that Haley and Todd could visit with Anne and Rick.

Once the kitchen was clean, I went to my room and grabbed my phone, shoving it in my hoodie pocket. I followed the laughter to the front porch.

"Do you mind if I go say goodnight to the horses?"

"Go for it," Haley approved.

"Say hi to Eddy for us," Todd added, then winked.

Sheesh. Am I that obvious?

"Who's Eddy?" Rick asked quietly.

"Her boyfriend," Haley answered.

I hesitated and then walked around the house, through the orchard and past the large tree, Spike at my side.

I didn't turn on the barn lights and could hear the soft crash of distant waves and the horses crunching hay. I looked at the phone.

It was 9:00. I wondered if Eddy was busy? Would he be mad if I called him? What if he didn't answer?

Oh, stop it!

I looked up at the sky and gasped. There were thousands and thousands of stars. It was nothing like the sky where I grew up. I stood for a minute listening to the chewing and staring at the glorious sky.

I held down the "2" button.

"Hello, my love."

My face was one big smile.

"Have you seen the stars tonight?" I asked. I heard a chair roll on his side of the phone.

He laughed. "No. I spent the afternoon with Paul. After dinner I hit the books. Big report due Friday. I can't mess it up."

"How's Paul?"

"His band was rehearsing and they wanted me to sit in."

"Are they any good?"

"Yes. But they need to practice. But I'll say this: They were better than the last time I heard them."

A door creaked open, then closed with a click. I wondered if someone had come into his room or just left.

"What did you do today?" he asked.

"Hung out with Haley. She can ride horses. It's amazing to watch her. Then we went to her surf shop. She owns a surf shop. Did I tell you that Todd is a cook?"

"You told me. I think he'd prefer to be called a chef, Babe. Horses? They have horses?"

"Big, huge horses. Where are you, Eddy?"

"Sitting in my backyard. Someone asked me if I had seen tonight's stars."

"Aren't they glorious? I've never seen stars like this or maybe I never looked."

"They're great." Eddy was silent for a minute. "So, you're good?"

I was sitting in the grass next to the barn. Spike put his head on my knee, I started to move away but decided not to. "For now, yes. I like it here."

"I'm glad," he whispered.

"Are you still picking me up next Saturday?"

"Of course. Something to look forward to. My parents want me to bring you back here for dinner. I was thinking we could walk on the beach first. What do you think?"

"I just want to see you," I said, wistfulness in my voice.

"Same here, Sam. Text me their address. okay?"

"I will. I'd better get back."

"I love you, Sam. I'll call tomorrow night."

"Okay. Hey, we're going clothing shopping tomorrow," I added, sounding excited even to my own ears.

He laughed. "Thank God!"

"Hey, be nice ... I love you, Eddy," I told him. After we hung up, I laid back on the grass to gaze at the stars. They were so close, I felt like I could reach up and touch one.

Chapter 18

"What are we waiting for?" I asked.

Haley and I were sitting at the island picking at a bunch of grapes. "Anne. She loves to shop and wants to come along. Oh, and here: This is a seasonal color chart," Haley told me, sliding a paper in front of me.

Before I had a chance to look at it, the door flew open. Anne bounced into the house wearing long sleeves and a big sunhat again. "Sorry I'm late. Are we ready?"

"Let's go," Haley said, picking up her keys and grabbing her purse.

"Where first?" Anne asked cheerfully as she slid onto the front passenger seat. She turned to me in the backseat and said "Ohhh, Sam, keep that skin out of the sun!"

"Did you make a list of what you need?" Haley asked.

"I started to, but decided it was easier to write down what I have."

Anne snatched my list and frowned, "This is all you have?"

"Yeah, it works."

"No, Sam, it doesn't work. I vote for underwear first," Haley said.

We walked into a store that carried nothing *but* undergarments. They were stacked on tables, hanging on racks, pouring out of bins. Haley walked straight over to a salesclerk and said, "She needs to be measured."

"Measured?" I eyed the lady walking toward me with a measuring tape around her neck. She pulled it into her hands and, before I could react, slid it around my body—first my chest, then my waist and, finally, thank God, my hips. I didn't care if I had to go without underwear the rest of my life; if she touched me one more time, I was going to scream.

The lady showed me a few different packages of underpants; I picked one. Haley tossed me a few different styles of bras. I went into the little room with a mirror on the wall and looked around.

Can *anyone see me?* I quickly clipped three bras on over my shirt. I took them off and left the room.

"I like these two," I said. Haley smiled and said, "Okay. Do you only want grey ones? I would grab a white one too." I did as I was told and watched Haley put the others back. She paid and we left.

"Good. That's out of the way. Now the fun stuff— hair!" Anne declared as we got into the car.

When we opened the salon door, the strong chemical smell made my eyes water.

"Sam? This is my friend Maureen," Haley smiled.

"Do you want to keep it long, honey?" Maureen asked as she brushed through my hair, flipping it this way and that.

"Yes, I think so," I said, trying to move so that Maureen's hands didn't touch my body. When she put her hands on my shoulders, I held my breath.

"Sam? I have to cut off at least three, maybe four inches, to get rid of all the damaged hair. See where the color changes? These ends are all damaged," Maureen explained.

Haley told her to go for it, and before I could say a word, Maureen had a towel around my neck and was leaning me backwards onto the edge of a sink.

After shampooing my hair, Maureen pinned up half and got to work. Haley and Anne sat on a couch in the corner reading magazines and glancing in my direction every few minutes.

The minute Maureen finished blow drying my hair, Haley and Anne dropped their magazines on the table. They stood in front of me with crossed arms and grinned.

My hair was just past my shoulders and not as thick, but the ends were now the same color as the rest of my hair. I opened my mouth to talk, but nothing came out.

"Do you like it?" Maureen asked.

"Yes." I ran my hands through my hair.

It's so soft.

"How do I make it look like this every day?"

Maureen tousled the hair on the back of my head. "Your hair is great. People would kill for it. All you have to do is wash it, brush it, and let it dry."

I didn't hide behind Haley when we walked around the shopping plaza, my new hair giving me confidence. The three of us shared a barbecue-chicken pizza at California Pizza Kitchen. After lunch, we shopped some more. One shop was wall-to-wall pajamas. There must have been hundreds of different patterns and styles!

Haley explained that with "jammies," the color wheel doesn't matter; they just have to make you feel comfy.

I got a silky, dark-blue pants set with horse heads on them and a soft-pink pants set with cute dogs on them.

Haley's new jammies looked fun. Hot pink splattered with light-pink hearts. Anne got a cream-colored nightgown with a design of white stars and moons. We picked out a cow-print flannel pant set that we all agreed Donna needed.

We spent hours trying on clothes, and by the time we got in the car to head home, I was tired of shopping. They seemed to be having a blast, but to be honest, I felt wrong letting Haley buy all this stuff for me. I decided to keep a log of everything they bought me because someday I would pay them back.

The car was packed. As I was starting to squeeze in, Haley said, "One last stop? Sam, do you want to get your ears pierced?"

I froze. "Will it hurt?"

"A little, like a pinch for a minute. What do you think?"

I was surprised to find Todd home when we got there. "Haley and I try to take Mondays off together. You got earrings, Sam! And I love your hair," he exclaimed. Todd pulled a few bags out of the back of the car and followed Haley inside.

Haley and I pulled item after item out of the bags to show him. He looked interested or at least he pretended well.

After dinner, I put my clothes away, careful to keep all the price tags until I could get some type of notebook. I stood back to look at the full drawers and closet.

I put on my new dog PJ's and checked myself out in the mirror.

It didn't look like me. Same face, but nothing else. I couldn't remember if I thanked Todd. I knew I thanked Haley. But Todd?

I took a deep breath, spun around and walked out of my room. The house was dark. A wet nose touched my leg, and I jumped and muffled a squeal.

Jeez, Spike!

I saw a glow under their door and tapped lightly.

"Haley? Todd? You awake?" I whispered.

"Yes. Come in," Todd called. I peeked around the door as I opened it. They each set a book down and looked at me with concern.

"Are you okay?"

"I just wanted to say thank you for everything. I mean, I have never had new clothes before and ... well, thank you."

"You're welcome." Todd said. As I backed out of their room, closing the door behind me, I overheard Haley say, "Can you imagine? She must have thanked me about fifty times. Todd, she didn't even flinch when they pierced her ears. It was almost like she knew it was going to hurt and shut down."

I tiptoed back to my room and closed the door. I turned on the light next to my bed and pulled out the book Haley got me today. A scratch at the door made me pause then get up and crack the door open. Spike walked in and jumped up on the bed.

The first week passed as we had agreed: I went to work with Donna each morning when she opened the surf shop at nine. I helped her open the blinds and set up a few things, then sat in the back office doing schoolwork. Haley arrived around 11:00, a few employees arrived around the time school was getting out. Donna and I would head back to the ranch around 3:30.

After dinner, Frank would look over the schoolwork I did and help me fix anything that needed fixing. Frank was a high school teacher, and he talked to the home-school board about getting me a heavy workload to "catch her up."

Haley's store reflected the passion she had for it. Employees were friendly and eager to work, the store was fully stocked with the latest trends—equipment and clothing—and the neighborhood kids gathered there after school.

While we were at the surf shop, Todd would check in at the restaurant but made sure he was home in time to make dinner. Todd said he really only had to be at the restaurant during dinner shift on Fridays and Saturdays.

Friday morning, I showered and prepared to go to work with Donna.

Haley was in the kitchen eating a bowl of cereal, a circle of dogs watching her every move.

"I was thinking," she said, staring into her bowl, "would you like to stay with me this morning and ride a horse?"

I stopped in my tracks. "I. Can't. Ride."

"I know that, Sam. I was going to tack up Luke for you."

LUKE?

My eyes popped out of my eye sockets and I had to blink a few times to put them back. "The big one?"

Haley took a last bite of cereal, got up and set her bowl in the dishwasher.

"Luke moves slow. Why don't you put on the jeans you wore yesterday to help me clean the stalls and we'll head out."

For a minute, I just stared at her putting on her riding boots and then I bolted for my room.

I must be crazy. She must be nuts!

I could feel my hands sweating as I pulled off clean jeans and slid into the ones I'd worn yesterday. I shoved my little camera into my pocket and headed back to the kitchen.

Haley handed me a baseball cap as we walked outside. She pulled Luke out of his stall and said, "You're getting good at cleaning these stalls. Sam, I need that cross tie." I handed her one of the ropes she used to secure the horses to the barn and she clipped it onto his halter.

"Start at the top and brush down," she instructed, handing me a stiff brush.

I looked at this massive creature. He towered over me; his head was at least the size of half my body! To brush his tan fur, I had to stand on my tiptoes. I started at his back, moving slowly down to his thick legs. When I got to his knee, he picked up his foot. I jumped back.

Haley laughed and said, "Good boy, Luke." She patted him on the shoulder. "When you run your hands down his leg, he'll pick up his foot so you can clean out his hooves. Just grab onto it."

She showed me how to scrape out the shavings, dirt and rocks. After she'd cleaned the back two hooves, she handed me the hoof pick and said, "You clean the front two."

I tried. She made it look easier than it was. His foot was the size of a dinner plate and heavy. When I finished, Haley tossed a square pad and cowboy-type saddle onto his back. She fastened the thick belt that held it around his belly.

Donna came out dressed in her work attire and announced, "Well, I'm off to work. Have fun, ladies. Haley, you both should wear a helmet."

Haley looked at me for a minute and nodded, then said, "See you around noon, Mom."

She pulled Abner out of his stall and put him in cross ties. She handed me the same brush and I started high and went down. Abner was not as wide as Luke and his legs were thinning.

"What type of horse is Abner?" I asked and Haley whacked those leg braces over her thighs before fastening them onto his front legs. "He's a thoroughbred. He wasn't the best racehorse, so I bought him."

"What's Luke?" I asked as I watched her carry a little pad and saddle out of the room where she kept all this stuff.

"Luke is Dad's horse and he's a Belgian," Haley answered, then added. "Belgians are a type of draft horse.

They're made to pull plows and carts. They're strong ... Abner is made for speed."

"Why is his saddle smaller? And there's nothing to hold on to," I asked, starting to annoy myself.

Stop asking so many questions.

"Luke's is a western saddle. This one is an English saddle, because Abner is a jumper."

Oh. Those boxes and gates are jumps.

Haley put a metal piece, which she explained was called a bit, into Luke's mouth, then had me climb up three steps. Luke moved next to the little steps and Haley said, "Okay, Sam. Put your left foot in here, grab the horn and toss your right leg over him." I froze.

Yeah, right.

She waited. Luke didn't move. After a long couple of minutes, I said, "Are you sure?"

"Yes, Sam. Just jump up."

I grabbed the horn, slid my foot into the stirrup, took a deep breath and flung the rest of me up onto this mammoth animal.

Haley tried to adjust the stirrups to my short legs. She finally gave up and had to punch another hole in the leather straps to make them fit properly.

"Walk around in here for a minute, Sam. I'll go get Abner and be with you."

"You're leaving me?"

"Don't worry. You'll be fine. And I'll be back in just a minute."

Hesitantly, I said, "Okay. Luke, go."

He didn't move.

I bounced up and down once. After trying a few more times, I asked, perplexed, "How?"

Haley laughed. "He knows voice commands. Tell him to "walk on" and squeeze him with your legs. Not kick, squeeze."

I took a deep breath, picked up the reins, and said, "Luke, walk on." He took a step, and my body tensed. With each heavy step he took, the ground shook. I swayed slightly as he moved his legs, but after a few steps, my body relaxed. By the time Haley got to me, I was breathing normally again, even smiling. She trotted Abner around the sandbox twice, then said, "Ready to go on the trail?"

I nodded. "I think so."

"So, pick up the reins and follow me around the arena first."

She taught me how to drive the horse. Once I was able to get him to circle the fences, we headed out of the arena. When Luke plodded onto the driveway, it sounded and felt like he was stomping the gravel into the dirt. On the other hand, rocks were flinging off of Abner's hooves.

I looked down.

Jeez. Don't fall!

We followed Haley out the front gate, across the street, and down a narrow, worn horse path. My mouth dropped when we emerged onto a sandy beach, waves crashing against the shore. Abner did a little dance. It looked like he wanted to run.

"What do you think?" Haley asked, a big grin on her face.

"It's amazing!"

"God has been good to us." Abner pranced a few steps, causing Haley to jolt forward, but she seemed fine with it. "He loves to run." she explained.

Abner calmed down after a few minutes. Luke didn't seem at all excited to be out here. We walked down the beach and then back, stopping at the path opening for one last look at the view. Doubting I'd ever find myself on horseback looking at the ocean again, I pulled out my camera.

Once back on the path, I asked, "Haley? Why do you thank God?"

"He created and gave all of this to us."

"But you and Todd work hard every day to pay for this stuff. Not God." Even though all I could see was her back on the horse ahead, I could tell she winced.

She looked back at me and said, "Well, I think you should read that book your boyfriend gave you. There are study guides to make it easier to understand."

I nodded and followed Haley back to the ranch,

I was elbow-deep in math when my phone vibrated. I answered with a grouchy "Hello."

"Well, hello, Sunshine," Eddy teased.

"Sorry. I'm trying to figure out this math. It's too hard."

"What math is it?" he asked. I flipped back a page and read him the title: Financial Math. Figuring out interest and balancing checkbooks ... stuff like that."

"Yeah, that can be confusing. Do you have to finish it today?"

I took a sip from my can of Coke. "No, but Frank wants to look this week's work over. And he plans to mail it back to the board on Monday."

"How 'bout I help you with it tomorrow? Math is my strong point. Is there another subject you can work on instead?"

I laughed. "Yeah. Hey, guess what I did this morning?"

"Learned how to rollerblade?"

"I forgot I told you I wanted to try that. Better. I rode a horse."

"Get. Out! That's great! Did you like it?"

"*Like?* No. I loved it. It was amazing. Best thing ever."

Eddy was quiet for a minute. I heard a car door close.

Oh no! Me and my big mouth. First, I offend Haley with my stupid God comment, and now Eddy.

"Eddy. Are you okay?"

"Of course. I just got to work. I wish I could have seen your face on that horse."

Whew. False alarm.

"At first I was scared, but not for long. I hope I can ride again. Hey. How was school?"

Eddy let out a big breath and said, "I turned in that big research paper. Thank God that's over! Hey, can I call you later? I have to clock into work." I paused a minute after we hung up.

Maybe I should have told him about my makeover. Naaa! Let him be surprised when he sees me—tomorrow!

Chapter 19

"Sam, it's 11:00. You better shower," Haley called out when she got out to the barn. The last three mornings I had helped Todd feed the horses, then I cleaned Lukes's stall and put him in his field while Haley took care of Abner. I loved it!

Today, Haley was dressed and ready for work.

"Thanks. I lost track of time," I said, putting away the pitchfork and walking toward the house. "Are you going to work?"

"I'm on the floor today. I have to be there at 12:30 so that Mike can have the rest of the day off. Todd is working late too." We walked in the back door, and she added, "Mom and Dad will be home all day."

"Yeah, I know," I acknowledged, taking off the muck boots and heading toward my room. I was in the shower when it hit me why she added the last sentence.

I slid into my jeans and slipped the navy camisole over my wet hair. Then I glanced at the clock: ten minutes to noon.

Eddy's close.

I brushed my hair and teeth again.

My heart jumped into high gear when I heard a light knock at my door.

I didn't hear the dogs barking. He's early.

"Sam?" Haley called through my closed door.

"I'm almost ready. Come on in."

Haley walked in and closed the door. I sat on the bed, slipping on matching socks and my new Vans.

"I came to help you get ready. I have make-up!" Haley grinned. She sat next to me on the bed and dumped out a bag.

"This is mascara, brown not black. It will complement your look, whereas black will stand out too much. The goal is to make it look like you're not wearing any makeup." Haley picked up a package and opened it.

"I'm going to have to touch you. Is that okay?"

I nodded, taking a deep breath.

"So, open your eyes and look up at the ceiling. It won't hurt."

She scooted closer and part of her hand rested on my cheek. I stiffened and held my breath; she paused a second, then smiled before she gently touched my lashes with the wand.

"Sam, breathe. This is eyeliner; the brush softens the liner. Almost done; now just some lip gloss," she murmured, applying the other items to my face. When she was done, I pulled on my button-up teal shirt, printed with outlines of navy flowers, and left it unbuttoned.

"How do I look?" I asked, pulling at the shirt and turning in a circle for her to see my outfit.

"You look great! Your hair's flat and sleek. Clothes fit properly and that shirt makes your eyes pop."

A smile slipped across my face.

"There is one thing," Haley said quietly.

"What's that?"

"Have you and Eddy? Um. Okay, I'm just going to say it: Have you guys had sex?"

"No." My face got hot.

"Okay, well, while you are staying with us, no sex."

"Yes ma'am," I said looking at my hands.

"Sam, you have so much to deal with right now. If he loves you as he says he does, he'll wait."

She stood up and smiled at me, then walked over to the door and left. I exhaled slowly and turned to look at myself in the mirror.

In this outfit and this haircut, I look like someone his parents would want *their son to date.*

The dogs went into a barking fit, paws went scratching across the wood floors and the front door opened. "Edward, please come in and sit down," I heard Todd say. "Sam's almost ready."

My palms started to sweat.

I grabbed my backpack and flung it onto one shoulder, freezing with my hand on the doorknob when I heard Eddy's voice.

"Thank you for letting me spend the day with Sam. You have a lovely house, sir." That made me want to run out of my room and hug him. But I was stuck.

What would he think of my new look?

"Thank you. What time do you plan to have her home?"

Home!?

"My parents expect me back by 11:00 tonight. If I'm not up for the first service tomorrow, there'll be hell to pay." Eddy laughed, and I smothered a giggle. "Will 10:00 do?"

Now I heard Haley's voice. "Absolutely. She should be ready. I think she's a little nervous."

"Nervous? About seeing me? She shouldn't be," Eddy said.

I started to turn the door handle.

"Well, it's been a busy week for her," explained Todd. "Eddy, we told Sam and we're telling you: No hanky-panky."

"Of course not, sir," Eddy said quickly.

That was my cue. I needed to get out there before they gave him a rundown on dating dos and don'ts.

The patter of my Vans on the wood told them all I was coming. Eddy's eyes scanned me as I walked toward him, but to be fair, I was checking him out too.

At the Center, he wore jeans and a T-shirt. Not today. His white T-shirt was tucked and belted into his loose carpenter khakis. An unbuttoned green-plaid shirt pulled it all together. He smiled when he saw me and my heart jumped.

"Wow. Sam, you look ... stunning," he declared. I laughed and twirled once in front of them all.

"Do you like it?"

He grabbed my hand and leaned in, and in a husky voice, he uttered, "No, I love it!"

"Well, I have to get to work. Remember what we said ... and have fun." Todd walked toward the door.

"Yes, sir, we will," Eddy responded, although his eyes were glued on me.

I went to pick up my backpack, but he grabbed it before I had a chance.

"See you tonight, Haley. Todd," I said. Haley was frowning and looking hard at the backpack on Eddy's shoulder.

"What's in the bookbag?" she asked.

"Oh, schoolwork. Eddy's going to help me with my math. Don't worry, Haley—I'm coming back."

Eddy added, "She'll be back by 10:00. I promise."

"Okay, well. Maybe I should get your parents' number, Eddy, just in case," Haley said, turning to grab the pen and pad by the phone.

Eddy wrote down a few numbers for her and we headed out.

"This is your car? What is it?" I asked, looking at the dark blue, two-door sports car.

He opened my door for me and said, "A Mitsubishi Eclipse. Yup, this is my car. Well, as long as I pay the insurance and car payment."

I started to get in the car, but he grabbed onto me and pulled me into a tight hug.

Jeez, he smelled good.

I started to stiffen then wrapped my arms around him and squeezed back.

"I missed you, Sam" he groaned, his face buried in my hair.

"I missed you too," I said. He finally let go, and I slid into his car.

The black leather seats were clean and the dash was dust-free. He tossed my backpack behind his seat and slid in next to me.

We drove down the driveway and onto the road in silence. "Did you wash your car today?" I asked.

He smiled. "No. Sam, why were you nervous to see me?" He reached for my hand.

"I look different. Mostly, I was nervous that you wouldn't show up."

"What? Sam, please!" His eyes rolled to the side. "I got you something. Open the glove box."

"But, no! I didn't get *you* a present," I said with a pout in my voice.

"Samantha. It's nothing, just—you'll get it when you see it."

I huffed and opened the glove box, then busted out laughing. "A box of chalk!"

He had a huge grin on his face. "A box of *multi-colored* chalk."

When we pulled onto the 101, he said. "Listen, I told my parents we'd stop by before dinner. Wait until they see the new Sam."

"Was I ugly before?"

"Ugly? You have always been beautiful to me. But with your new hair and clothes? Babe, you are stunning."

I watched the ocean.

"Eddy?"

"That's me." He glanced at me, the corner of his lips turning up into a grin.

"Yesterday morning, Haley and I went for a ride on the beach. She said God gave her everything she has. I don't understand. All four of them work. Why do they give the credit to God?"

He swallowed hard and turned down the stereo.

"Did you read my book yet?"

My face got hot and my voice louder. "NO! She wouldn't answer me when I asked her either ... Why do I have to read that? Can't you just tell me?" I turned to look out the window.

"Sam."

"Never mind," I grumbled. He turned off the highway and pulled into an empty beach parking area. I watched him get out of the car, walk over to my door, then open it. He offered me his hand. I looked at his hand for a long minute before taking it. He closed my door and leaned back against his car, pulling me to him.

"Don't get mad at me, Sam. I will answer your questions. It's just that I don't think you'll understand my answers."

What?

I clenched my teeth but resisted taking a step back. "I. Am. Not. Stupid! " I declared, tensely.

He loosened his grip for a second, shook his head, and pulled me back into him.

The gold chain around his neck rose and fell as he breathed. I struggled to calm myself.

I hate letting him see me upset! Damn! He thinks I'm stupid!

He put his hand under my chin, pulling my face up toward his. "I never have and never will think of you as ugly or stupid. Do you hear me? Jeez! How do I explain this?"

He slid his hands into my back pockets and looked past me, like he was looking for the right words somewhere in the ocean.

"Just say it," I demanded, still angry.

"I meant that you would not understand the reasons; I didn't mean you weren't *capable* of understanding His Word."

I stared at him.

"Sam, please. Don't be mad at me. No one has taught you about God, His love, His promises. So how can you understand our love for Him? But, you see, it's something you have to read and figure out on your own."

He bent his knees to look me in the eye. Then pulled one of his hands out of my back pocket and ran his knuckle down my cheek. "Don't be mad. Take a breath."

I closed my eyes and whispered, "Help me understand, then."

He kissed me softly before speaking softly into my ear. "Gladly. I will."

"Ready?" Eddy said as we pulled into a driveway. Through a line of trees, I saw the huge white house.

"This is your house?" I exclaimed, with wide eyes.

He laughed. "Well, my parent's house. But, yes, I live here."

It was two stories high with a huge, covered porch that stretched across the front of the house. Big white pillars held up the porch roof, and the six windows above the porch had window boxes overflowing with flowers under them.

He parked the car in front of one of four garage doors and got out. I paused a minute, nervous that his parents were waiting for me to walk in.

"Are they home?"

Eddy took a step and wrapped his arms around my waist. "What are you worried about? You've met them before."

"This is different. We're in the real world now."

He gave me a quick kiss, took my hand, and pulled me toward the front door.

He stopped before he opened the door and raised an eyebrow, as if to say, "Ready?"

I nodded, and in we went.

"Mom! Dad! We're here!" he yelled. A little tan and white dog ran up to us. Eddy bent down and ruffled his big stand-up ears. "This is Whiskey," he said as he put the dog down. I got down to my knees next to Whiskey and asked, "What happened to his legs?"

Eddy laughed. "What do you mean? He has legs ... don't you, Whiskey?"

He looked kinda like a German Shepherd with his legs cut off, just body, ears and paws.

I grabbed onto Eddy's arm as we walked into a huge living room. White walls and cream-colored furniture, it looked more like a museum than a house. The coffee table was glass with a fan of magazines displayed on it. A vase of fresh flowers sat on each of the two glass end tables.

I slid my hand down his arm and Eddy linked our fingers.

"Mom?" Eddy called, as we walked into a large kitchen. "Wanna drink?" Eddy asked.

My mouth fell open.

Todd would love to cook in here.

Black cupboards lined two walls and formed an island. There had to be thirty cupboards. Around the island were five metal bar stools that matched a table at the other side of the kitchen.

"Come on." He headed back the way we came.

"What's in there?" I asked as we passed closed double doors.

"The formal dining room."

"Formal?"

He stopped walking to give me another hug.

"We only eat in there when we have important company."

"Do you have a lot of parties here?"

"We have a lot of pool parties during the summer. On Christmas and Easter, we have family celebrations here. I want to check my dad's study before I assume they're not home."

He headed toward the stairs and opened the door next to a big white wrap-around staircase. This room was different. A brown leather sectional faced a massive TV. One wall was lined with book-filled shelves. Eddy's parents sat on the couch and stood up as soon as they saw us. I squeezed Eddy's hand hard as we walked over to them and tensed up when they hugged me.

"Wow, Sam. What a transformation! You look great!" his mom said, her eyes big as a bug's. She tilted her head as if looking at me from a different angle would bring the old me back.

"Thank you," I mumbled. Whiskey jumped up on the couch and Eddy's mom smiled big and asked, "Did you meet our wee boy?"

"I sure did," I uttered and I pet "the wee boy" again.

"She asked me where his legs went," Eddy said, and his parents laughed.

"He's a corgi, so they're supposed to look like this," his dad explained.

"Where's Paul?" Eddy asked, looking around the room.

"With the band. He'll be home soon," his dad offered.

"What do you two have planned?" his mom asked, sitting on the couch and tapping the spot next to her. I slowly let go of Eddy and teetered on the seat next to her.

"I plan to take her to dinner. I might be a few minutes late getting home; Sam has to be home by ten," Eddy told them.

"No problem, honey. So, Sam, where are you going to dinner?" his mom asked me.

"He won't tell me. Your house is beautiful," I stated.

"Thanks. We like it. What's your new home like?" she asked kindly.

I pushed my hair behind my ears. "Very nice. It's a ranch," I explained.

The front door slammed. "Mom! Do we have anything to eat?!"

"That would be Paul." Turning to me, Eddy asked, "You wanted to meet the punk?"

His dad shook his head and his mom frowned. I told them it was nice to see them again as we headed out the door.

I followed Eddy into the kitchen. "Paul!" Eddy exclaimed.

"What?" Paul had both refrigerator doors open, as well as the doors to cupboards, so that I could see piles of neatly stacked white china inside.

"Paul. This is Sam."

Paul stopped making his sandwich to look me over once and then went back to his meal. "Hey, Sam! Nice to meet you."

Paul was not as tall as Eddy and he was dressed head-to-toe in black.

"How was practice?" I asked, sitting at the island.

Paul's face lit up. "Great!"

Eddy put away the food Paul had left on the counter and closed all the doors. He leaned against the sink and watched Paul and I talk. As soon as the sandwich was gone, Paul gulped his soda and left the kitchen with a casual, "See ya later."

"I told you, Eddy sighed. "He's a punk. Come on, I'll show you the upstairs. Then we have some math to do."

At the top of the steps, I looked down to see the living room and kitchen.

Cool house! So cool!

Eddy pointed to an open door, "That's the bathroom if you need it. Paul's room is over there." He pointed to a closed door, out of which came blasting music. At the far end of the hall was a double door. "That's my parent's suite."

"This is my room." He turned and walked into a room across from his parent's and I followed.

There were shelves full of books along one wall. "Did you read all of these?"

He closed the door and said, "Yep."

Across from the bookshelves was a big bed covered with a gray and black comforter, a huge poster-sized picture of ice being sprayed by skates was above it. A wall of windows was on the opposite side of the door.

I stood at the floor-to-ceiling windows, admiring the view. The backyard was neatly landscaped around a kidney-shaped pool that had a waterfall at the far end. Past the pool was a little cottage, then the ocean.

I heard Eddy kick off his shoes and walk across the room. He wrapped his arms around me from behind, and I leaned into him.

"This is amazing," I said, watching the waves in the distance.

He kissed my neck softly. "Uh-huh."

I turned to face him. He took a deep breath and ran his hand down my back to pull me close. I reached up on my tiptoes so I could kiss him. He kissed me gently at first, then more insistently. I reached my arms up to wrap them around his neck, and he picked me up off the ground, holding me tight as we softly kissed. He carried me to his bed and laid us down. I held my breath as he kissed to the edge of my shirt, his breath on my skin as he hesitated above my camisole for a minute.

"No hanky-panky. Right?" he whispered.

"Right," I groaned. He kissed from my camisole up my neck to my lips. "I promised my parents," he said, rolling off me to sit up. We agreed that we needed to leave this room before we didn't care what promises we had made.

We worked on my math in the kitchen. I tried to ask him about work and hockey, but each time he nailed me with: "Focus, Sam—you can do this."

"You're not going to make me try raw fish, are you?" I asked. I looked out the car window at the restaurant sign. Eddy got out and opened my door.

"Never." he smiled, reaching for my hand.

"I can't speak Japanese. How will I know what to order?" I asked with anxiety when he opened the restaurant door, letting me in first.

They sat us with strangers at a U-shaped table. There was a big flat grill in front of us, with seven plates framing it. I bit my lower lip.

"What? You can't speak Japanese. Neither can I, let's just leave."

Eddy winked. "Calm down, Sam"

Eddy ordered some sort of scallop and steak dinner. I looked for something safe on the menu. Chicken and steak. That would work. But when the waiter set chopsticks on our plates, I stared at Eddy, "Are you serious? No forks?"

What have I gotten myself into?

Eddy slid my napkin aside, and there was a fork. "These are more fun," he said, lifting his chopsticks and tapping them together.

A man with a big chef hat rolled out a cart loaded with raw vegetables and uncooked meat and scallops. He checked the heat on the grill.

The chef greeted us then started to toss veggies onto the grill. He chopped broccoli, carrots and onions. The grill sizzled, as he started slicing the steak into strips. I could not help but smile as he sang songs and tossed eggs into his hat, even making a volcano out of onion. The flames shot a foot high! The chef had everyone try to catch a shrimp in their mouth, but of course, I wasn't willing to try. I had never had shrimp and was not about to vomit in this restaurant!

The chef set some fried rice on our plates, and I looked around to see if I was supposed to start eating or wait for the rest of the food. Eddy moved his plate closer to him, picked up his chopsticks, and poured some pink sauce on the rice.

"Try it," he urged smiling, pointing with those chopsticks. I tried to take a bit of rice using those silly things, but the rice just fell on my new shirt. I scowled at the plate. Eddy snorted a laugh and then took a scoop of his rice and fed it to me.

"Oh, wow, that *is* good!"

"See that pink stuff?" He pointed with his sticks. It's shrimp sauce. Or yum-yum sauce. Pour some on the rice and try again. It acts kind of like glue. Plus, it tastes great." With that, he took another bite. I did as instructed, mixing the sauce into my rice. Then the chef set chicken and steak on my plate along with some veggies. I worked at the chopsticks again and was able to pick up some of the vegetables. After some practice, I managed to eat a little of the rice, too. But I ended up just using my fork.

I stared at Eddy in amazement. He had eaten his entire meal with chopsticks.

"That was great! I can see why this is your favorite place to eat. Thank you, Eddy, for taking me," I said sincerely as the car came to life.

"You are most welcome. We have about half an hour before we should head to the ranch. How about a walk on the beach?"

I hesitated for a minute.

"Would you mind if—. Well, can you take me back to the ranch?" I said softly.

His smile faded and he looked hurt. "You want to go home? Are you not feeling well?" he asked, focusing his gaze on my eyes.

"No, nothing like that. I just want to show you something at the ranch," I assured him, lifting his hand from the gear shift and pressing my lips against it.

"Whew!" His color came back, and he leaned across the car to kiss me.

When we pulled up the ranch driveway, the house lights were on.

They waited up for me.

Eddy opened my door and pulled me into a hug.

"Eddy, since they're up, we should go say hi first."

We went inside without knocking, but I paused when heads shot up.

Crap. Should I have knocked?

"Hey, I didn't know you guys were coming over," I said, noticing Anne and Rick.

"Yes, well, we, uh ... wanted to keep Haley company," Anne said. I smiled.

Right. They're keeping Haley company. Yet, she doesn't strike me as the type to need company.

"This is Eddy," I said, waving my hand toward him. Eddy reached over me to shake their hands. "Eddy, this is Anne and Rick. They live next door.

"What do you think of the makeover?" With both hands, Anne drew an imaginary outline around me.

"She looks utterly beautiful," Eddy winked, and my cheeks flamed up.

We sat with them and talked for a few minutes. They asked him the typical questions about school, then college, where he worked and all about his family.

I saw Eddy glance at his watch then at me with a frown. "Do you have five minutes?" I asked, standing up.

"At least five," he grinned.

"Haley, do you mind if I show him your horses?"

Haley smiled at the two of us.

"Not at all. I stopped at the store to buy more carrots. Someone has been feeding them a lot lately. Would you grab the bag out of my car and take it to the barn on your way?"

"Yes, ma'am," Eddy said promptly. We headed toward the kitchen.

"Very put-together young man," I heard Rick say quietly.

I looked back at Eddy. His face had turned hot pink. So, he *could* blush like I did!

"She has so much to overcome. Don't you think they're awfully young?" Anne asked.

"Yes. But, his parents assured us that he's not playing a game with her," I heard Haley say.

I started to grab the carrots out of Haley's car, when a long arm reached over me. Eddy picked up the heavy bag with one hand, then grabbed my hand with his free one.

"Lead the way," he ordered, grinning.

I flipped on the light. The horses blinked and stuck their heads out of their doors.

Eddy stopped in his tracks. "Jeez. They *are* huge."

I smiled, remembering my own first impression and took two carrots out of the bag before Eddy set it in the box.

I shoved one carrot in my back pocket and snapped the other in half. Then I took Eddy's hand, flipped it over, and set the half carrot on it. He tilted his head and just looked at me. "Open your hand like a plate and the horse will take it. It's so cool!"

Eddy didn't flinch as the large creature's teeth came at him. Luke's lips pursed out and took the carrot without even touching skin. A huge smile formed across Eddy's face as he shoved his hand toward me for the other half. After we had petted both horses, and the crunching stopped, I shut off the lights and started toward the house. Eddy grabbed me around the shoulder and pulled me back.

"Wait, Sam. I have a few minutes."

I snuggled into him and looked up at the sky; my stars were still there.

"This is where I called you from the other night," I told him. We stood silently for a few minutes.

"They're so bright. I wonder if it's because we're far from the city. Sam, listen, I can't make it out next Saturday," he said, still looking up. "My hockey team made it to the playoffs, and if we win Saturday morning's game, we play again Saturday afternoon. If we win that, the championship game is Sunday afternoon. I was hoping to come get you Sunday morning, but my parents are already on me because I'm playing hockey on a Sunday and hockey doesn't come before God." He scoffed, and I turned to look at him.

"Well, don't push it with them. Sounds like an important game. Maybe Sunday, after your game, you can have dinner here. I'll ask Haley and Todd."

He kissed me for a second and then checked his watch. "Times up. My mom teaches a ladies' Bible group. I'm going to talk to her so that I can answer your questions correctly. I mean, I know why I thank God, or as you see it, give him the credit. I want to make sure I don't mess it up."

I nodded. "Okay."

When we got to the car, he pulled me close and set his forehead against mine. "Let's run away," he said, closing his eyes.

"Okay, next Sunday," I whispered, and he kissed me. We both laughed.

"I love you."

"I love you more," I said, and he snickered.

"That's *my* line."

"Is that right?"

He straightened his back. "That's right. I'll call you tomorrow," he said, cupping my cheek with his hand. One last peck on the cheek. As he drove off, I watched his taillight get smaller.

When he pulled out of the gate, I bounced into the house. It was dark. The only light was coming out from under Haley's door. I went to my room, washed my face, and brushed my teeth. I slipped into my horse PJs, but as soon as I slid under the covers, there was a scratching sound at my door. I peeked out in time to see Spike shove the door open with his nose to let himself in. He jumped up and lay down on the end of the bed, looking up at me.

I climbed back under the covers and let my feet rest against him. The contact felt nice.

It was just a dog, but I wondered if that meant I was getting better.

Chapter 20

"I'm ready," I said, walking out of my room to the kitchen island. I reached between Donna and Haley to grab a cluster of red grapes.

"Haley and I took the morning off to take you to see a boarding school."

My stomach flip-flopped, and I fought back the urge to bolt for my bathroom.

What have I done wrong? Why do they want to get rid of me already?

I felt numb. If they were going to dump me, I wanted to say goodbye to Luke. "Oh. I'd like to stop out at the barn before we leave," I said casually.

"Sure. Dad is mailing your schoolwork today. He checked it over and said everything looks good," Haley said cheerfully.

I nodded and dropped my head. No way did I want her to get a hint of what was going on in my mind. I spun on my heels and yanked open the door. The sound of it slamming behind me made me jump.

The horses were still in their stalls. I grabbed a carrot out of the tack box and approached Luke's stall. By the time I was halfway there, he had flung his head out to greet me. I snapped the carrot in half and offered him a piece. His lips tickled my hand. I reached up and stroked his mane. The barn was peaceful—its quietness broken only by the steady rhythm of Luke's chewing. I giggled when he nuzzled my pocket looking for the other half.

The sound of Haley's voice startled me. "Are you ready to go? Todd's ready to put the horses out."

"Yep. I'm ready."

I didn't say a word the entire car ride. Green fields scattered with cows, and horses flashed by the window. Haley drove through a valley where mountains loomed on either side of the car, the ocean view getting smaller and smaller.

We turned onto a single-lane dirt road. All I could see were miles of field on both sides of the narrow road. Brown dusty cows stood in clusters under the few shady trees that broke up the rolling hills.

My heart went into high gear when Haley pulled into the tiny parking lot of a camp that looked like it was out of the hippy era. I froze when they got out of the car.

Are they going to ditch me here? Why didn't I think of this before we left the house? I forgot my phone. All I have are the clothes on my back.

I took a long, slow, deep breath, squared my shoulders and got out of the car.

A man in Birkenstocks, shorts and a T-shirt walked out of a wood-framed building and shook hands with Haley and Donna. If he said hi to me, I didn't hear him.

They talked for a few minutes before he introduced himself to me as Mr. Jackson, the director of the school, and offered us a tour.

I stayed between Haley and Donna as we walked around the campus of wooden buildings and dirt paths.

Are they really going to leave me here?

"These are the girl's quarters. There are four girls to each cabin. On the other side of the campus are the boys quarters. We have fifty cabins total, with about 190 students currently attending," Mr. Jackson informed us.

We glanced inside the one-room cabin at two sets of bunk beds and four desks.

Haley turned and started walking and I was quickly at her side.

"Here are the dining room and kitchen; the students do all the cooking in cabin rotations."

He explained each building as we poked our heads inside. All I could think about was how the hell I could get out of going to this school that reminded me more of a camp.

The last building we went to housed the offices. He handed Haley a packet of information and turned to me. "I hope you will be joining us soon."

Haley and Donna shook his hand. I bolted for the car and was sitting in my seat before Haley and Donna were out the main door. My heart leapt out of my chest with each beat and I whispered to the empty car, "I don't want to leave the ranch yet."

Instantly, I was angry with myself for even wanting something that I knew could never happen.

Don't you dare start to love them, I warned myself. *They're getting rid of you too.*

Haley and Donna got in the car and both turned back to look at me. Donna's eyebrows shot up.

"Samantha? Are you okay?"

I nodded but could feel that all color had drained from my face. My heart was beating in my ear.

Haley looked at her mom then fired up the white SUV.

The ocean air started blowing through the vents as we drove toward the ranch. Haley stopped at a sandwich shop for lunch. By then, my color was back and my heart was beating at a normal pace. After all, I was heading back to the ranch ... for now.

"Well? What did you think of that school?" Haley asked, taking a drink of her diet Coke.

"I don't know. Do you want me to go there until I leave for Nebraska?"

Haley frowned and said, "No silly. We were thinking instead of Nebraska. You looked scared out of your mind. What was going on in your head?"

I picked up my sandwich and said, "I thought ... nothing. I just didn't understand."

I couldn't tell them I was afraid they were going to ditch me.

Donna reached across the table to set her hand on mine. "Sam. We were not going to leave you there. You know that right?"

I pushed down the dry burn in my throat with a quick gulp of my kiwi-strawberry Snapple and picked up a piece of green noodle.

"What is this again?" I asked.

"Pesto pasta with sundried tomatoes. It's good; try it," Haley encouraged.

"That was never the plan. We just wanted to explore some other options. We all agree sending you to *any* state-type home is a waste," Donna added, taking a bite of her salad.

Haley took a bite of her sandwich and let her eyes roll back. "This sandwich is amazing. Side Street Café does it again!"

I ate slowly, took a bite of the pasta then a bigger bite, adding a sundried tomato.

This is good.

Anne and Todd were sitting on the front porch when we pulled up the driveway.

"Well? Is it a go?" Anne asked, a glimmer of hope in her eyes.

"I don't think it's right for Sam," Haley said in a matter-of-fact voice.

Todd followed her into the house.

"Do you want to spend the rest of the day with Rick and me?" Anne asked.

I had started heading out to the barn, but her words stopped me cold. "Do you want me to?"

"Of course, silly! You can help us with our clothing line. Did I tell you that I'm a clothes designer?" Anne rambled. As we walked into the house, I could hear Todd and Haley talking in their room.

I froze. I waited for a pause in their conversation before I called out, "Haley? Todd? Anne wants me to spend the rest of the day with her. Is that okay?"

"Wait. We want to talk to you first," Todd answered. Their door opened and I took a step inside. Their room was a lot like mine except for a set of French doors across from their king-sized bed and the blue-plaid comforter.

Todd tossed a floral pillow against the driftwood headboard and sat on the bench at the end of the bed to tie his shoes.

"You do understand that we want to help you. Right?" Haley asked, coming out of the bathroom. She stood in the doorway, slipping on earrings.

"Yes. Thank you," I replied, not quite sure how to respond. She took a deep breath and shook her head. I stepped back a step to look at the bookshelves on either side of the French doors.

I would love to get my hands on one of those books.

"Have fun with Anne. I'll pick you up after I check in at the store," Haley smiled. She turned back to the bathroom and it looked like her shoulders dropped. Todd gave me a fake smile and shrugged.

Anne and Donna were on the deck, but they stopped talking when I walked out of the house.

Jeez! I hate that.

Donna told me to have fun as she walked up the steps to her house. I followed Anne onto the brick path. We walked past Frank's chicken coop and his greenhouse.

I hope he shows me his birds before I have to leave.

Anne unlatched their back gate and held it open for me.

"Come on in. Rick! Sam is here!" she called out. We walked across a small tidy garden and into their home.

I set my backpack on a tan chair in the living room and followed Anne into the white and brown kitchen. She offered me a drink, but I shook my head.

Rick came in and said, "Well, to what do we owe this honor?" He leaned against the counter and crossed his arms.

"I thought Sam could use a break," Anne said. She pulled something that looked like mashed bird seed out of the refrigerator, set some crackers on a plate, and handed it to Rick.

"Do you want to help me?" he asked, gesturing toward the hallway.

I tilted my head to look. There were four open doors in the hallway. I had no idea what he had in mind and my head was starting to ache. I stood there biting my lip.

Rick said, "Come on. I'll show you what we do." I followed him slowly. We walked into a room with rows and rows of brown shirts, all exactly the same. He set the crackers and mushy stuff down on a table. "Here—eat this while I tell you about our project."

I picked up a cracker and scooped a tiny bit of the mush on it. "What is this?"

Rick laughed. "Sorry, kiddo. I should have explained. That's hummus—mashed chickpeas."

When I made a face, he said, "Give it a try. I think you'll like it." He pulled out a magazine and flipped to a tabbed page. "See? Anne designs a clothing line. These shirts need the final touches before we ship them out."

I looked at the book and then at the rows of brown shirts.

Rick handed me a container of button covers that had flowers hot-glued to them. "Can you clip these over the top three buttons for me?"

I nodded, set the plate down, escaping having to have a bite, and got to work.

Haley walked over to collect me after she went home and changed. Before we left, Rick asked if I wanted to help out a few days a week. He even offered to pay me. Of course, I said yes. My own money!

On the way back to the ranch, Haley asked what time Eddy would be picking me up tomorrow.

"He can't make it tomorrow. Playoffs. He's going to try to pick me up on Sunday unless he has a game."

"Well, you can hang out with one of us."

"Sure. Will you take me to buy a notebook? Like the ones for school?" I asked, ashamed to be asking.

They give me so much.

"Of course!" Haley said, as we passed Frank and Donna's house,

I'd heard Frank say, "Just enroll her in school. Get her in school!"

"I think they forgot we're out here," I ventured. "I'm so cold!" We were huddled on the back porch and my teeth were chattering.

The morning dew was starting to roll in. "Me, too, Sam," Logan stuttered. "Maybe we should see if a window is open." We stood up and looked around the backyard.

Just then two men hopped over our back wall, landing on their feet like cats, and started to stroll toward us. We froze.

"What do you want?" Logan shouted as the dark figures got close.

They stopped, and we took a few steps back. I put my hand on the doorknob and twisted. It didn't move. "Please leave us alone." I tried to sound stern, but my voice was shaking.

It was too dark to see their faces. They had large, bulky builds. When they started to laugh, we both stiffened, too cold and frightened to run. One guy flicked his cigarette toward us, the other lunged forward ... NO!

I sat up and gasped for air.

Okay. Okay. I'm safe.

I looked around the room and wiped my forehead with my jammie sleeve.

I wish Eddy was here.

The alarm clock glowed red: 3:12. I picked up my phone, took a deep breath and then set it back down.

"Sam?" Haley called gently.

Shit! Shit!

"Yes?" I groaned.

She cracked open the door. Her hair was uncombed and wild.

"What's going on? We heard ..."

"I'm fine," I snapped, not meaning to.

"Okay ... well, do you want to talk?"

"No. I'm good. Thanks," I said, lying back down.

"Spike! Up!" she called. My door clicked shut and something landed on my bed. I almost jumped out from under the covers until I saw Spike curled up at my feet, which moved down to rest against him. Afraid to close my eyes, I picked up my phone and sent a text.

"Sleep well, Eddy. I love you."

I held the phone in my fist and slowly closed my eyes, but within seconds, the phone hummed.

"Why aren't you asleep?" the screen said.

"I will be soon. Spike just curled up with me," I typed.

"Lucky Spike."

Chapter 21

"She's adorable!" the pastor's wife told Haley while I fidgeted uncomfortably in my church dress. "She's lucky to have you," she continued.

"Yes, and we're lucky to have her," Todd replied before he headed into the church. I followed like a good little duckling.

Sitting between Donna and Haley, I listened to a man talk about God and Jesus; he might as well have been speaking Chinese.

Are God and Jesus the same person?

Since we're at church, I decided to have a private conversation with God. Between me and Him.

I'm going to do everything these four are asking me to do, which means I will sit here and behave, but you need to know something. Every time a social worker would take us away, we would sit and listen to them trying to find us a foster home and they would smile at us, offer us snacks and say, "God has a plan." Soooo, if your plan for me was Stacy, then I don't trust you. If your plan for me was to be hungry, cold and scared ... I don't want to know you. If your plan for me was to be hit, touched and hated ... Well, guess what? I hate you!

"What time is Eddy's game?" Todd asked as we walked into the crowded Woodland Hills Ice Rink.

"2:00," I answered, spotting Eddy's mom and brother standing in front of double doors.

Mrs. Pattin greeted us with a smile and hug.

When he saw us, Paul pulled open a door. "There you are! The game is starting soon—Dad's saving us seats." Paul was taller than his mom, but not as tall as Eddy.

Icy air rushed out of the building, and a shiver ran through me. Todd and Haley slipped on hoodies as we walked into what felt like a freezer.

Why didn't Eddy tell me it was going to be so stinkin' cold?

Dr. Pattin was sitting in the middle of the stands. I weaved through the crowd, careful not to bump into anyone on my way to the five empty seats beside him.

"Oh, Sam—Edward asked me to give this to you," his mom said. She picked up a zip-up hoodie and handed it to me. I set it on my lap and stared at the sheet of ice. It was surrounded by hip-high walls topped with thick glass that reached almost to the ceiling.

"How will I know what's going on?" I asked.

"You'll catch on. When lights and buzzers go off, cheer," Todd mocked.

I shivered and looked back at the empty rink, suddenly remembering the hoodie. I flung it around my shoulders, taking a deep breath as I slid my arms in the sleeves. The scent of Eddy's cologne with shower gel made me forget that we were packed in the stands like a can of sardines. His scent comforted me. I smiled.

He knew I would be cold. He's so sweet!

As I was zipping up the hoodie, a bunch of skaters ran onto the ice. The sardines all started to cheer.

The skaters all looked the same. Black helmets and pants, orange jerseys and orange socks. When they had circled half of the ice, another set of skaters, these in blue jerseys and socks, ran out and started to circle the other side.

"How do you know which one is Eddy?" I asked, narrowing my eyes to see if I could spot him.

"Look for the blue jersey with "24 Pattin" on the back," his dad said over the stir of the rowdy crowd.

The orange team started to hit little black things across the ice to each other. I scanned the blue Jerseys.

"There he is. See? Talking to the goalie," his mom pointed. Eddy and the goalie knocked fists, then Eddy took off across the ice.

"What is that black thing he's hitting?"

"A puck," Todd said, without taking his eyes off the action on the ice.

The skaters rushed past the stands, and I fidgeted in my seat, trying not to wave like a lovesick chick.

"Sam," his dad said, trying to keep a straight face, "he won't look up here. Edward gets into a mental zone and focuses only on playing."

I jumped when a loud buzzer went off. All the players bolted across the ice to climb over the hip-high wall.

Three men in black-and-white-striped shirts skated onto the ice and blew a whistle. A few players jumped back over the wall and stood in the middle of the ice. Each blue jersey had an orange jersey facing it.

Eddy was in the center. Stick down, head up. The referee dropped the "puck" and two sticks fought for it. "So they fight over the puck?" I asked, not taking my eyes off the ice.

"Yeah," Todd whispered to me.

When the puck shot across the ice, I lost track of Eddy. Blue and orange streaks raced across the white ice. Every once in a while, two players would slam into the glass and fall to the ice. Then they would jump up, racing to the puck.

The coach was yelling from the bench. I couldn't hear him, but the players must have. They all either went faster or dove over the half-wall to trade places with players.

Buzzers went off. Lights flashed. People stood up and cheered. It was fast, loud and exciting.

Haley and I gazed intently at the ice. Someone watching us would have thought we were going to write an article on the game.

"The first period is almost over. I'm going to get coffee. Want anything, ladies?" Todd asked, starting to get up. We both shook our heads, afraid that we might miss something.

Three guys slammed into the glass with a loud thwack. Haley and I both cringed.

Owwww!

A long buzzer announced that the first quarter was over. Todd and Dr. Pattin came back with coffee and hot chocolate.

A machine was gliding across the ice. With each pass, it turned the scuffed ice into a sleek glass.

The second and third quarters were just as exciting as the first.

When the game was over, Eddy's mom stood up and stretched her arms. "Good! They won!" Her smile was so big, her eyes looked squinty.

Eddy's teammates were jumping on each other, butting helmets and laughing.

"Would you like to come to our house and join us for dinner?" his mom asked as we lined up to leave the stands.

"Sounds nice!" Haley responded.

"Sam. Wait!" Paul said, looking at his cell phone, "Eddy wants me to take you to him." I paused, hoping for Haley and Todd's approval. "We'll wait here," Todd said, his mustache unable to hide a knowing look.

I followed Paul down a long hall. He pushed through a swinging door, and I stopped. The ice was right there, less than four steps away.

"Don't go over on the ice. Come on," Paul urged.

I shoved my hands in the hoodie pockets and followed.

"Good game, bro," Paul said as we walked beside the low wall. Eddy's black padded pants were held up with suspenders. The jersey and top pads were gone. "Thanks, little brother."

Eddy took my hand. I couldn't believe how warm his hands were. Just looking at his sweat-soaked T-shirt and wet hair made me shiver.

"Aren't you cold?"

He laughed. "Nope. Did you wear socks?" He knelt in front of me.

"No, my toes are numb."

Eddy grabbed a bag off the bench and pulled out a pair of socks, then slipped off my clogs.

"What are you doing?" I whispered, trying not to draw any attention.

He fought back a smile as he slipped a sock on my right foot and grinned at me. "I'm taking you ice skating."

I started to pull my foot away, but he caught it. Without lifting his head, he raised his eyebrows and rolled his eyes up to meet mine, as if to say, "Trust me!"

I knew there was no need to tell him I couldn't skate; he already knew. Two guys jumped on the ice and started to race around.

"You have five minutes, Pattin," his coach commanded.

"Thanks. Hey, Coach. This is Sam," Eddy said, sliding a skate onto my foot.

I reached out and shook his hand.

"Nice to meet you, Sam. Have fun. Remember: five minutes."

Eddy stood me up. Wow, was he tall with those skates on! I wobbled and reached for him as we moved onto the ice. I shook my head.

"I can't believe you're making me do this. I'm going to fall," I said, a bit of panic in my voice.

The guys whizzed around us.

"That's Joe and Shaun. I'll kill them later. Sam, do you really think I would let you fall?" Eddy asked, wrapping his arms around me and dragging me to the center of the ice. I closed my eyes tight and leaned back into him, letting my skates glide under my feet.

It has to hurt to fall on this ice.

After a minute, he whispered in my ear, "Breathe. You won't fall. So why were you up at three this morning?"

I slowly let out a deep breath.

"No reason. I just couldn't sleep."

He loosened his grip and I tensed up and grabbed his hand. "Don't worry—you were practically skating on your own. See?"

He let go, and I was sure I'd fall. But I didn't. I was skating! Kinda. More like step, step, glide. And Eddy ... Eddy was skating backwards.

How does he do that?

I looked down at his feet to see what he was doing that made him go backwards and promptly stumbled into his arms. We both laughed.

"Baby, don't look down. It throws your balance off."

He locked eyes with me.

"Sam, don't lie. You had another one of those dreams, didn't you?"

I shrugged.

"Times up, Superstar," Joe, or maybe it was Shaun, yelled across the ice. Eddy shook his head and pulled me to the bench. The ice machine started up again.

"What is that?" I asked.

"It's called a Zamboni. It makes the ice smooth for the next game." Eddy glanced at the ice then started to untie my skates. "How often are you having nightmares?"

I started biting my thumbnail. He pulled off the skates and slipped my clogs back on my feet.

"No answer? Well, I have to get changed. Paul, can you take Sam back to Haley and Todd?"

"Yeah. Mom told me to tell you to hurry. Everyone is having dinner at our house."

Eddy nodded and they both walked away.

Eddy's mom set an etched-glass pitcher of lemonade on a long patio table.

Todd and Eddy talked about the colleges Eddy had applied to and what schooling he needed to be a neurosurgeon. I watched the waterfall flow into the pool behind Haley. Its trickling and the shooshing of the waves on the beach behind the house were relaxing and my mind drifted off until someone said, "Sam, have you looked at colleges?"

College? I haven't even been to high school!

"What do you want to be?" Eddy's dad asked.

I could feel everyone looking at me. The hair on the back of my neck stood up. "I haven't thought about it."

All I'm good at is taking care of my sisters.

Haley scoffed, "Oh please. If you could do anything, what would it be?"

"Well. I would want to help people. No. Kids. I want to help kids," I murmured.

There! I answered your questions. Paul's turn?

"Like a child psychologist?" Eddy's mom asked. I wasn't going to get off the hook that easily.

"Yes," I said, then shook my head. "No. Those are kids who someone is already trying to help. They're already safe or on the way to being safe."

Eddy picked up my hand under the table and laced our fingers. I squeezed.

"Like a nurse. Someone in direct contact. Someone who, for the four to five hours that kids are at the emergency room, makes them feel cared for. Someone who understands the fear in your eyes as the doctor stitches you up or puts your bone back in place. Someone who realizes that when they're done fixing you ..."

My voice was starting to crack, but I wanted to finish what I had to say. I cleared my throat and continued. "... you are going to be sent home with the person who has just broken you—but, for that moment, you are in loving arms. You are safe." I poked at my half-eaten dessert.

"See? I told you she's a diamond in the rough," Haley exclaimed.

Todd smiled.

I rolled my eyes.

"What about you, Paul?" I asked in a desperate attempt to get the attention off me.

"I'm going to be a rock star," Paul stated, pretending to play a guitar.

Dr. Pattin rolled his eyes and his mom shrugged. But the rest of us cracked up.

Once dinner was over, Eddy and I took our plates to the kitchen and then went into the living room. He pulled me onto his lap and hugged me close.

"Thanks for coming to my game," he whispered into my neck.

"It was interesting. I've never seen a hockey game before. To be honest, I wouldn't have imagined you played something so ... rough."

"I told you it—relieves stress."

He said it with a slight laugh before his lip stiffened and his eyes met mine. "So, how often, Sam? How often do you have nightmares?"

"Don't worry about it," I replied and started to get up, but he didn't let go.

"I do worry, so spill it."

I rested my forehead on his. "Every time I close my eyes, I see things you don't need to know about. Okay?"

"I want to know everything about you," he said, sounding almost hurt. "Why don't you trust me, Sam?"

"You're the only person I do trust. Please don't be upset. There are parts of my life ..." I trailed off.

No way am I putting shit about my past in his head.

He took a deep breath and gave me a quick kiss. "When you're ready to talk about it, I'm ready to listen. Did you read what I asked you to read?"

I frowned. "Yes, I did. And I went to church today. They might as well have been speaking Greek. I don't get it. Aren't God and Jesus the same person?"

He muffled a laugh. My eyes opened wide—I didn't see any humor in my sincere question.

"Sorry ... I'm not laughing *at* you. Each church or religion has different views and it can get complicated, but—"

"If it's complicated for you, how do you think I feel? Can you at least explain why everyone keeps thanking Him?"

Eddy shoved his hair back. "Okay, the important thing is that all things are possible if we trust God, and without Him we would have nothing. That's Matthew 19:26 and it's important."

"Oh, well, *now* I understand," I said sarcastically, with a toss of my head and a roll of my eyes.

"Please read those verses again. Ephesians 5:20 tells us to give thanks to God always for all things and the Father in the name of our Lord Jesus Christ. I wrote down the page for you. Read it, then call me."

I nodded, but he continued to stare at me. First, he raised his left eyebrow, and then he tipped his head like he wasn't sure if I heard him or not.

"Yeah, I heard you. I'll read the highlighted paragraphs again. Jeez!"

Haley walked into the room and spared me from any more discussion. She ran her hands over the top of a big black grand piano in the corner. "Your mom said you can play this beautiful instrument."

"Yes, ma'am, I can," Eddy replied, moving me off his lap to get up.

He pulled some music books out of the bench, set them on top of the piano and waved his hand over them. "Pick one."

Haley glanced at the sheets and handed him a booklet. Eddy's eyebrows almost touched his hairline. He spread four papers on a stand in front of the keys and sat down.

We stood next to the piano and I watched his long fingers glide over the keys. As I studied his intense face, he stared at the white pages with black lines and dots in front of him. We all listened as he played the piano, just like we were at a concert.

His mom smiled with pride as the rest of us were stunned silent.

Chapter 22

"How often does she do this?" My eyes popped open to see who was talking.

"I told you, Mom, every night," Haley answered. They were outside my door.

Crap!

"Maybe. Should we take her to see Dr. Sue or Melanie?" Todd asked.

I sat up and looked at my alarm clock.

Shit! 4:20 in the morning!

"No. Dr. Sue said Sam wouldn't talk about it with her, plus they would just want to medicate her. No," Donna sighed.

"Maybe she should call Eddy; she trusts him," Frank suggested. I held my breath and wiped the sweat off my face.

"She does but she needs someone trained. You know, when Spike is with her, she doesn't scream, she still talks, but this is a bad one. That's why I called you guys," Haley said.

"I'll make some calls in the morning and find her a therapist here," Donna said.

Someone started to turn my doorknob, and I crumpled into the wet sheets.

"Spike. Up! Stay! Good boy!" Todd whispered. My door clicked shut. The bed sagged when Spike jumped up and plopped his head on my feet.

Once the house was silent again, I sat up and flipped on the lamp next to the bed. Spike looked at me, so I gave his head a pat and reached for the spiral notebook under my phone.

I took two deep breaths before flipping to where a pen held the next empty page, pausing to look at my phone. The alarm clock's bright red "4:32," stopped me from holding down the "2." I ran my hand over my collarbone. There it was; the evidence of tonight's nightmare. I picked up the purple pen and started to write:

How do I tell anyone that I can still smell the cigarettes burning my skin? It is a smell and a pain that no matter how hard you try to, you can never forget. How do I tell anyone something like that? And why would I tell someone who has only read about it happening? They have no clue!

So I just don't.

The waves were crashing against the shoreline as Luke and I walked down the path. I could see Haley and Abner prancing around in the damp sand ahead.

"You're very quiet today. What's up?" Haley asked when we finally came to the end of the path. She motioned to me to turn Luke and head down the beach.

I shrugged. "Just thinking. If I go to that school you showed me, will you guys visit me?

She stopped Abner.

"I mean, it might not be so bad there. Maybe better than Nebraska, like ... I'll still get to see you guys, right?" I asked plaintively, walking Luke up to Abner.

Haley squinted out at the water.

"And Eddy would be close," she offered.

"Well, yeah. That too. But he's applied to colleges near Boys Town. In case you haven't noticed, he's very, what's the word—? Driven."

Her eyes met mine.

"I ... I'm gonna miss you guys, and if I go to that school, I can still see you." I looked away, wishing I had kept my mouth shut.

"The thing is, Sam, this has to be a group decision. A few factors are involved. As a ward of the state, you might *have* to go to Nebraska. Health insurance, you know adult crap, but Mom has made some calls to see if there are options. So, just know that Mom's working on it."

I nodded, gave Luke a light kick and took off.

The smell of the ocean and the sound of hooves in the sand gave me time to think.

I wanted a fresh start, but maybe I don't have to go as far away as Nebraska.

Haley and I were silent as we took the leather off the horses, cleaned them up and put them into their fields. I looped the halter and lead rope on Luke's fence and stood back as he stomped away.

"Sam?" Donna's voice startled me.

"Oh, Donna, sorry I'm not ready. Can you wait ten minutes? I'll hurry," I said, starting toward the house.

"No, wait. It's okay, Sam. I made an appointment for you to talk to someone. A therapist. Haley will take you— today. Go get cleaned up," she instructed.

Shit! I don't want to talk to anyone!

"Oh, okay." I put my head down and headed to the house, kicking up gravel as I went.

Haley was still in the shower after I was dressed, so I grabbed my new packet of school stuff and sat under a tree in the orchard to work on it. Well, I tried to work on it. But I just couldn't concentrate—so, instead, I watched the horses grazing.

"Sam? Let's go. Mom said we'd better be on time."

I shoved my work into the backpack and got to my feet.

"Where are we going?" I asked.

"Mom called a therapist and he's squeezing you in during his lunch break."

I sighed.

"I'll come in with you—but, Sam, do you want me to come into the session with you?" Haley asked, as we pulled up to a small white house.

"You don't have to," I said in a flat voice, looking at the tidy covered porch. I didn't look back as I walked up to the office.

The house had been turned into a doctor's office and what should have been the front room was the waiting room. I looked around, deciding where to sit. I frowned at a man sitting in a chair in the corner. He was asleep and he had a bunch of needles sticking out of his feet.

The lady sitting next to him said, "Oh, don't worry, dear. He's just getting his acupuncture. It doesn't hurt a bit."

I took a seat on a couch, facing a fireplace in the middle of the room. Before Haley had a chance to sit down, a thin, dark-haired man walked into the room.

"Hi, Haley. This must be Sam. I'm Dr. Dunn."

He shook hands with both of us and then asked us to follow him. He led us through the kitchen, out the back door, down a brick path, and into what looked like the garage. The inside had been finished off and turned into an office. It reminded me of Dr. Sue's office at the Center, except the couch was red. He sat in a chair next to the couch and Haley walked over to the desk.

Huh? Bet they expect me to sit on that couch. Dream on!

I walked over and looked at the photos that surrounded his desk.

"Sam, do you know why you're here?"

"Nope." I pointed at a photo of him holding up a big fish. "When did you catch this?"

"Last summer. Sam. Please sit down," he said nicely enough, but it was clear that he wasn't going to take no for an answer.

So, I sat—barely—teetering on the edge of the couch.

"Your family is worried—"

"They're *not* my family," I interjected.

Haley sucked in air.

I knew I was being a brat, but I couldn't help myself. After all, they were getting rid of me.

"In a way, you're right. But they are related to you. And Donna and Haley are worried about your nightmares."

"Why? They're not contagious."

He raised his eyebrows.

"Sam!" exclaimed Haley. "I have never seen this side of you." Haley leaned back and hugged herself with her arms. "You're ... hostile."

I scooted back into the couch and crossed my arms, trying to get it together. She was right; I was being very rude. I sighed.

"I'm sorry."

Dr. Dunn nodded "It's fine. You've been through a lot. But we'd like to help you. What are the nightmares about, Sam?"

"I don't want to talk about them. I don't see the point."

"Do you dream about someone hurting you?" he asked.

As usual, I shrugged.

"Sam, we want to help you figure out these nightmares. If you can figure them out, you might stop having them."

"You can't help me. I have them figured out."

He jotted down a few notes and then asked me about my sisters and brother. We talked about what I liked here and what I thought about going to Boys Town. When the hour was almost up, he asked me to wait for Haley in the waiting room. Before I could sit down, she was back and ready to go.

It was a quiet ride home. Before I got out of the car, I said, "Sorry I was mean, Haley. Thanks for taking me to see Dr. Dunn."

"Anytime, kid. He's an asset, and you'd be wise to use him. I imagine you'd feel better if you stopped having those dreams."

She has no idea—every time I close my eyes, I want to scream. Like it's as easy as talking about it and they go away. Whatever.

Haley and I spent the rest of the day together. Cleaning stalls. Weeding the garden. Then we met Frank and Donna at Shoreline Beach Café for sweet-pea soup. The soup looked nasty and I only tried it to be polite. But after the first sip, I had to stop myself from licking the bowl clean.

I curled up in my bed that night wishing I wouldn't have been so mean to Dr. Dunn. He was just trying to help. I decided that if I went to see him again, I'd be nicer.

"I'm going to clean the stalls," I told Todd and Haley.

"We'll save you pancakes," Todd nodded.

I put on my ball cap and slid my hair through the back. I put Luke's halter on him and, as I led him to his field, I saw Haley marching past the oak.

"Are you going to ride?" I asked.

"No. Not today ..." A sneaky smile slid across her face. "... but Abner needs his workout. Do you want to ride him?"

I froze. "What? I can't ride him!"

"Nothing fancy. I'll stay in the arena with you." She handed me a brush and went to get the English saddle from the tack room. "Todd and I are going to L.A.

overnight to visit his family. You can spend the night with Mom and Dad. Eddy's going to be here soon, right?"

"Yes." A big grin escaped onto my face.

I watched her wrap Abner's front legs and then put his tack on. It was so easy for her; I wondered if I could ever be that good with horses.

When Haley handed me a helmet, I felt all color leave my face.

"He moves differently but trust me: He will *not* hurt you."

The butterflies in my stomach turned into bees as I walked up the steps at a crawl.

Stop it, Sam.

I shoved my foot into the metal stirrup and flung my leg over him, wobbling, because there was nothing to grab onto—no horn on an English saddle.

Haley took a few minutes shortening the stirrups while Abner fidgeted. He was ready to go.

"Shove your heels down. Stretch your leg as long as you can," Haley directed. She moved my foot so only the ball of it was in the stirrup.

"Squeeze him with your calves. Like a tube of toothpaste. Your legs are the gas. Hands are the breaks."

He moved away from the pressure of my calves. If I pushed with one leg he moved away from it. He didn't sway when he walked but bounced. And when he bounced, I bounced. What a difference! Compared to Abner's gait, Luke was stiff.

After about an hour, Haley said, "Time to hop down. I have to go shower so I look beautiful for Todd's family." She gave me a wink. "Can you groom him and put him in his field?"

When I finally lowered myself off the horse, my legs felt like Jell-O. The dogs followed Haley into their house.

"I wish I could stay," I told Abner. "I'm going to miss you."

As I brushed his coat, I watched Haley and Todd pull out of the drive. I took my time walking Luke to his field. When we got there, I hung up his halter on the horseshoe hook and watched him start to graze.

When the dogs ran to attack Eddy's car, I remembered the first time I pulled up this driveway and giggled. I left my room to greet him.

"Hey, lady!" he said, pulling me into his arms.

"Hey. Do you wanna say hi to Frank and Donna?" I asked, flipping my freshly washed, wet hair into a bun.

"Not really. I want every minute with you." He let go and grabbed my hand. "But lead the way."

Donna and Frank were getting ready for a Costco run.

"Frank. Donna. Do you remember Eddy?"

"Of course." Donna gave him a hug and Frank shook his hand.

"Frank, can you show us your birds?" I asked.

"Sure! By the way, I looked over your schoolwork and it's going in the mail today. Well done, kiddo!"

Eddy shot me a "Whoa, look at you!" glance and we followed Frank past his house to the bird area.

I told Eddy about the time I spent with Frank as he fed and watered his feathered friends. He spent over an hour showing us the row of walk-in cages, each one with a different species. Frank stepped into each cage and put seed in the feeders while telling us about the birds.

"These are my favorites, the peach-face lovebirds. But I sell these finches the most, although these cockatiels are the best pets."

Eddy and I walked to the car and followed Frank and Donna off the ranch. They went north, we went south.

We decided to stop at the beach after lunch. Eddy pulled over at a spot where there weren't many surfers.

We sat in the sand and Eddy wrapped his arms around me, resting his chin on my head.

Waves crashed against the shore, and I leaned my back against him, watching birds with long beaks and long legs poke around the wet sand.

Frank didn't have any of these.

"Have you ever surfed?" I asked.

"I tried it once, but cold water, seaweed and sharks aren't my thing."

"So! There's something you aren't good at?"

His laughter made my body jiggle. "I am not good at a lot of things, Babe."

"Hmm."

He kissed the top of my head and whispered, "Are you doing okay, Sam?"

"I think so. They took me to see a private school the other day, in the middle of nowhere. I think they want me to go there instead of Boys Town. Ohh, and then a therapist."

"What?"

"They took me—"

"—I heard you." He shifted his weight. "When? Where?"

"The school? Last week. It's somewhere behind that mountain. I thought they were going to leave me there."

"Are you going there instead of Nebraska?" he asked, with a hint of excitement in his voice.

"At first I told them I didn't want to. I wanted to go to Nebraska. I want a fresh start—"

"—But does your fresh start have to be in Nebraska?"

I turned to face him. "Jeez! Just listen."

"Sorry. I'm all ears." The crease between his eyebrows got deeper.

"No. I *could* have a fresh start here. Haley said she would make some calls but, for now, I belong to the state, so I have to go to Boys Town in a week."

"But if they say they want you to stay and go to that school, will you?"

"I don't know. I'd rather live with them, but I think they want my me to live at that school."

We looked at each other for a few minutes. Eddy pulled my hair out of the bun and tucked a few stray pieces behind my ears.

Then he stood and shoved his hand down to help me up. Once on my feet, I wrapped my arms around him. He hugged me back and said, "Hey, have you ever been to the zoo?"

"The zoo?" I laughed.

"Yes. You know lions, tigers, elephants, monkeys. The zoo!"

"No, can't say that I have."

"Well, that's a crime. Santa Barbara has a cute little zoo. Let's go!" he enthused, pulling away and grabbing my hand.

We spent the afternoon walking from enclosure to enclosure, stopping at each one to watch the animal in there and read all the educational boards. I pulled my disposable camera out and took photos of a few things ... until it stopped: I'd used all the film. Eddy put it in his pocket, telling me that he could take it somewhere to get the photos printed.

On our way out of the zoo, we saw one of those photo booths. The one where you pick a frame, then sit inside, making faces and laughing as you quickly find the next pose before the light flashes. We printed two and walked hand in hand to the car. He opened my door and kissed my forehead before I sat in the passenger seat. We stopped at In-N-Out burger and ate in the car.

He took a few bites before saying, "Well, which was your favorite animal?"

I thought about it for over a minute, then answered, "The sea otters. What about you?"

He didn't hesitate. "The gorilla. He's badass! The signs said they could lift 1500 pounds and are eight times stronger than a human man. Like bad ass! Why the otters?"

I took a bite and then a drink. "They played with that ball and kept bringing it to the glass to show everyone. Then I was reading the sign, and it said that when they sleep, they hold hands so they don't float apart. So cute!"

"Oh, yeah? Well, Sam, I'll hold your hand when we sleep, because the last thing I want is for us to float apart."

Chapter 23

"Are you ready *yet*?" Haley yelled into my room. I stopped packing and looked at the clock.

"No," I called back. "I thought I had plenty of time!" I bolted from my room and through the kitchen.

This is my last day here, I want to take my time and enjoy every minute.

Todd had the car running while Haley was holding the rear passenger door open for me. I climbed in next to Donna, and Haley slid in beside me.

"Sorry. Where are we going? My flight doesn't leave until tonight." I said as Todd pulled out the gate.

"We're taking you to lunch," Frank declared.

"Oh. Great. Only, I want to feed the horses and see Eddy before I leave."

Haley's mouth curled up at the corners and she looked at her window. "I promise you'll be able to see Edward today."

Todd parked and I said "Manny's?"

Frank nodded and we all jumped out. The restaurant was quiet and brightly decorated. There were Mexican hats on the wall and saddles or plants in each corner. The hostess led us to a booth in the corner and set five menus down. Our waiter came over and set chips and salsa on the table. We all ordered water and started to look at the menu.

"What are you getting?" I asked Haley.

"Hmmm. I think the shrimp tacos," she answered, before taking a chip and dipping it in salsa.

I listened as everyone ordered, then as if I'd known exactly what I wanted to order, I announced, "Chicken tacos!"

Nice and safe.

We asked each other basic questions as we ate, visiting like the family I had gotten used to over this month. We were all being careful not to bring up anything to kill our final meal together.

I'm leaving tonight. Who's picking me up from the airport?

After the server cleared our plates, Haley ordered a fried ice cream "With five spoons, please."

I have to admit, I was interested to try fried ice-cream. We had talked about trying one the first time we came here to eat, but we were so full when we were done eating that we didn't.

I was excited to try it, after all ... the carrot cake that Todd made was glorious!

Will I go to restaurants in Nebraska? Where will I eat at Boys Town? Sam, stop!

Our waiter set a whipped-cream-loaded bowl in the middle of our table. We each grabbed a spoon, then paused.

Who's going to break the shells?

Todd pointed his spoon toward me. "Sam? Would you be interested in discussing alternatives to Boys Town?"

My mouth dropped open. I closed it and then opened it again. "Yes!"

Todd shoved his spoon into the crispy fried ice cream shell. Suddenly. I didn't want any; my stomach had gone to knots. He filled his spoon and took a bite, then set his spoon on a napkin.

Haley loaded her spoon. "Well. The four of us met with Dr. Dunn yesterday—wow, this is a good one, Sam. Dig in!" Haley said, interrupting herself.

"You were at Anne and Ricks," Donna explained, taking a small well-planned bite and pushing the bowl toward Haley. "And we needed an objective opinion."

Frank frowned and pulled the bowl to him with his spoon.

"The way we see it, Sam, you have three options," Frank went on, taking a huge spoonful.

I have options?

Unable to resist any longer, I plunged my spoon into the caramel-covered ball. "But Nebraska's a fresh start for me," I offered. Todd and I watched Haley's spoon plunge in for the perfect mixture of crust, caramel and ice cream.

"Yes. Nebraska is. So, option one, you get on that plane tonight. If you need anything, we, of course, will be a phone call away." Todd said, scooting the bowl toward me.

"Option two is the school you saw. You would stay there Sunday night to Friday night, then one of us would be willing to pick you up every Friday and take you back."

Todd stopped and looked into my eyes, like he was trying to figure out what I was thinking. I nodded to break his stare.

"So, I could be with you all on the weekends?" My shaking hands scraped the bowl with my spoon.

"Option three. Well, option three is you, um—you live with us," Donna grinned.

My eyes brimmed with tears.

NO! Don't you dare cry!

"You would have to go to school, of course," Frank stated.

"Why? Why do you want me now, but you didn't before?"

Who cares why?! Tell them you want to live with them!

"Sam, your mom has told everyone that you are demon possessed and a white witch with powers to do evil. While we didn't believe that, we were concerned about what would cause a mom to say those things. Darlene assured us that you were none of that and to give you a one-month trial," Frank continued.

Shit! Why does she say those things about me?

"After we met you, we realized you were just a teenager. Sam, we can't send you to a state facility; it's not right. But the choice is yours," Donna concluded.

I squeezed my eyes tight to hold back the tears. There were so many thoughts whizzing through my head and so many feelings fighting inside me. I wished Eddy were with me—he could have helped me figure this out.

NO, he would say this is a no brainer!

"Sam, please think out loud," Haley sighed. "Help us understand what's going on in that head of yours."

I smiled. Swallowing a hard hot lump in my throat.

"I want to stay with you guys so bad, but I want a fresh start too. No one knows me in Boys Town. They don't know what I have been through or what my mom thinks of me. Being there would give me a chance to figure out who I really am." I took a deep breath and let it out slowly.

I love it here.

"Well, Dr. Dunn said it best. He compared you to a rose garden that was planted, but never weeded or fertilized. The tall weeds are preventing the roses from reaching their potential. The rose leaves are brown and the petals wilted. Weeds are stopping the roses from growing to their potential. All the roses need is to be weeded, trimmed and fertilized. We want to help you grow. What do you think?"

In spite of my efforts to maintain control, a tear snuck out of my eye and down my hot cheek.

"You've all been telling me that I had to go to Boys Town. What if I do something wrong? Will you send me away then?" I choked over the lump in my throat.

"Oh, Sam. We wouldn't want to, but, well, it depends mostly on you," answered Haley. "We have a list of rules. I told you we would make some calls and that I didn't know if we could keep you here. Mom and I talked to Darlene. She worked out a way for you to either go to a private school or— stay with us."

"So? What do *you* want, Sam?" Frank asked.

I glanced at each of them. *This was a big decision. Probably the biggest decision.*

Something Eddy had said popped into my head. "If they offer to send you to that school, what will you do?" My answer was "I don't know. I would rather live with them."

Here's my chance. Oh, God, what if they end up hurting me? What if they decide they don't want me in a few months. What if—

"Sam, this should be an easy call for you. Think about it this way. Do you know how lobsters are caught?" Todd asked.

My eyebrows knitted together. "No clue."

"Lobsters?" Haley scoffed.

"Fishermen go out in big boats. They attach their traps to chains and tie the bait to the bottom of the trap. There's a hole on the top. The fishermen toss a line of traps into the ocean," Todd explained. "The traps float down to the ocean bottom and, once the sand settles, the lobsters climb up the traps and drop inside.

"After a few hours, the fishermen start to pull up the chains and the lobsters try to climb out of the traps. But, instead of helping each other, they grab onto each other, pulling each other back inside. As a result, they all get caught. The point is, Sam, don't let anyone—or anything— pull you back into the trap."

A silly grin crawled onto my face, and I snagged my lower lip with my teeth in a failing attempt to stop it.

"I want to live with you guys!" I declared, making sure to glance at each of them before adding, "Please?"

Frank nodded and looked at Donna. She smiled and patted my shoulder. Haley said, "Wise choice, Cuz."

Todd pulled a folded paper out of his back pocket.

"Good. But first, we want to discuss a few rules," Todd said. The paper crackled as he opened it.

"Okay. New rules?"

"Some. Yes. You will attend school every day. This year is almost over, so Frank talked to the school board. You can continue home studies and start in the fall. We'll help you get closer to your grade level," Todd said.

I nodded. *School, check!*

"No drugs. No drinking. No smoking." Haley said.

No problem! I can do that.

"Sure!" I agreed, although I was not sure that this was for real.

"Every Friday, you'll see Dr. Dunn for an hour. You must be home every night by 9:30. And you will continue to be nice. Sam, we go to church on Sunday. You don't have to believe it, but we will expect you to attend," Donna continued.

"Last, but most important," Todd added, "no one from your past is to have contact with you. Sam, that includes the girls and Logan. We know this is a hard one, Sam," Todd said, without looking up from his paper.

"We just don't want anyone to know where you are. But we'll take you to visit your sisters one more time, so you can make sure they're alright. They will need to be told you are going to Nebraska, the next day" Donna added, in a sad tone.

I ran my sleeve over my storming eyes.

Did they really just ask me to join their family? But give up mine?

"My girls?" I asked in almost a whisper.

Logan will be fine. But my sisters?

"Yes … As far as everyone will know, you went to Boys Town. I'll take you to see the girls next week. Then they'll be told that you're gone," Haley said gently.

"This is a deal breaker, Sam. Time for you to focus on you. Darlene will set up a time when you can see them to say goodbye," Frank intoned in his firm-teacher voice.

I nodded, staring at the paper in front of Todd.

"Any questions?" Todd asked.

"Yes." My voice cracked and I had to clear my throat before I could continue. "Am I still under watch?"

They glanced at each other. "Watch is over. You've earned that," Todd said.

I don't want to push it, but this one's a deal breaker for me …

"What about Eddy? He's important to me." Suddenly feeling brave, I added, "And, hey, can I get my own dog? I need a big dog."

By now, the tears were seeping uncontrollably, but I didn't care. They were happy tears.

All four of them laughed. "Yes, of course you can still see Eddy. We talked about it and decided that depriving you of Eddy would be like depriving you of food. But no sex. It complicates things and you don't need that right now." Haley smiled.

By this point, the ear-to-ear smile I had was threatening to wrap around my head!

"About the dog," Donna chimed in, "let's give it a few months. If things are still going well, I think we can find room for another dog."

"Research what type of dog you would want, maybe get a summer job and save up to buy it and pay vet bills … That way, it will really be your dog," Todd added.

"A big dog would be good for you. Maybe, I can have mine back," Haley said with a smile that matched mine. We all chuckled.

I thought about my new status on our way home. Someone actually wanted me! No, not someone: four people. Four people wanted me to be part of their family. I babbled on about everything and nothing. They couldn't have shut me up if they'd wanted to.

Todd and Haley had their life just as they liked it, with no kids to worry about. They were free to do whatever they wanted and were willing to give up some of that freedom for me.

I unfolded the contract that Todd had drawn up. **"Our Girl"** was written in bold letters at the top.

Wow! That's me!

The three options were typed neatly, followed by a list of the rules that applied to each of those options. Option number three was circled, and in Todd's handwriting above the five signatures were two amendments to option three: (1) Sam can get an after-school job to purchase the dog of her choice. (2) Sam can continue to see Eddy, who also must adhere to the set of rules established above.

I put the neatly-folded paper in my back pocket. As we pulled into the driveway, Todd and Frank looked at each other.

"Are you going to talk to the young man or should I?" Frank asked. Donna craned her head around Frank's shoulder and giggled.

"I'm ready for him," Todd acknowledged.

There was Eddy, sitting on the front porch steps petting one of the dogs.

"Can I talk to him first?" I asked.

I had to wait to get out of the car, since I was lodged between Donna and Haley. I think they moved slowly on purpose. I was aching for an Eddy hug.

I walked toward him and watched as my new family disappeared.

Eddy wrapped his arms around me, then handed me an envelope and said, "Your photos, m'lady."

"Thanks ... did you look at them?"

He shrugged and said, "Yeah. What time is your flight? Do we have time to go somewhere?"

"Yep! Plenty of time," I grinned. "Want to feed the horses some carrots with me?" We started to walk toward their fields and I stopped.

"Oh. This is from my mom."

He pulled a small box out of his hoodie and handed it to me. I opened it. A cute little silver bear necklace was inside. I smiled and exclaimed, "I love it!"

He laughed. "She said the head and arms all move, so it reminded her of you. Never holding still."

I snorted a laugh.

I was having a hard time hiding the grin that had taken over my face. Not the "I will be okay" smile that normally lived there, but an "I *am* okay" smile that was genuine. I pulled the paper out of my back pocket and Eddy asked, "Your sisters?"

I looked at him with affection and said, "Nope." I pushed it toward him.

He took it. "Oh, your flight plan ... is your new addr..." He paused suddenly as he opened the page.

He read it for a minute before his eyes met mine and he grinned. "You get to stay here?!"

I grinned bigger and nodded.

He picked me up in a bear hug and we both laughed with delight as he spun me around before setting me back down. He kissed the top of my head and handed me back the letter.

"They want me! Oh and, Eddy, Todd is waiting to talk to you."

"Sounds good."
I turned and looked around.
I was home.